Society American Tract

Lyntonville

The Irish boy in Canada

Society American Tract

Lyntonville
The Irish boy in Canada

ISBN/EAN: 9783744740722

Printed in Europe, USA, Canada, Australia, Japan

Cover: Foto ©Andreas Hilbeck / pixelio.de

More available books at **www.hansebooks.com**

LYNTONVILLE;

OR,

The Irish Boy in Canada.

PUBLISHED BY THE
AMERICAN TRACT SOCIETY,
150 NASSAU-STREET, NEW YORK.

CONTENTS.

4   CONTENTS.

CHAPTER IX.

CHAPTER X.

CHAPTER XI.

CHAPTER XII.

LYNTONVILLE.

CHAPTER I.

LYNTONVILLE.

"Thou who hast given me eyes to see,
And love this sight so fair,
Give me a heart to find out thee,
And read thee everywhere."

LYNTONVILLE was the name of a large
old-fashioned log-house which stood em-
bosomed among the tall trees of a Cana-
dian forest, where sombre balsams and
hacmatacs mingled their dark foliage
with the silvery birch and maple. Delicate buds and blossoms peeped out from
beneath their rugged stems or uprooted
trunks, and feathery ferns lurked in hidden nooks and corners in the woods all

around it. There too the squirrels frisked about, and the little chip-muncks chirped merrily as they played at hide-and-seek among the branches.

"The house itself was of timbers
Hewn from the cypress-tree, and carefully fitted
   together.
Large and low was the roof; and on slender columns
   supported,
Rose-wreathed, vine-encircled, a broad and spacious
   verandah,
Haunt of the humming-bird and the bee, extended
   around it."

Mr. Lynton had been settled in this house in the woods for many years. It was the birthplace of all his children; and though most of them were now married and had homes of their own, they all loved to revisit the dear old house where they had spent the happy days of their youth. Harry, the youngest, was the last chick left in the nest, and he was not a whit behind the others in his affection for his beautiful home.

Mr. and Mrs. Lynton were well known and highly esteemed in all the country round; and before the neighborhood had attracted so many settlers, Mr. Lynton had acted for many years as clergyman, lawyer, and doctor to the whole district. He was a good naturalist too, and the hall at Lyntonville was full of curiosities, and was famous in that part of Canada as a museum of natural objects. Harry Lynton inherited his father's tastes; and it was his great delight to discover a rare insect, or bird, or flower, which might be added to its treasures. This hall was a large, square room, into which the front door opened; it had been originally intended for a parlor. Several other apartments surrounded it, and opposite the entrance was a large open fireplace, where the great logs were piled in winter, and blazed away cheerily up the wide chimney. A deer-skin lay in front

for a rug, and several stags' heads, ar-
ranged according to their ages by the
branching antlers, looked down from the
wall over the oaken mantel-piece. Large
cases of bright-colored birds were there,
all of which Mr. Lynton had himself shot;
aye, and stuffed too with his own hands.
In one corner was a cabinet of butter-
flies, moths, and beetles; in another, a
bristling porcupine stood in an attitude
of defiance. Here a racoon curled himself up in close imitation of life, and there
a snarling wolf showed his cruel white
teeth. Spreading fungi stood out like
huge brackets from the wall; in short, it
were vain to attempt to enumerate all
the wonders that were there. In the
long winter evenings, especially about
Christmas, when the children used to
gather around the great hall fire, and ask
"grandpapa" for one of his marvellous
hunting-stories, the little ones would cast

furtive and fearful glances at the wild
animals, which seemed so life-like in the
flickering firelight; or would look round,
half expecting to hear the wild war-
whoop issue from the hollow garments of
the Indian chief in the shadowy background.

But there were even greater attrac-
tions for Harry out of doors. A swift-
running river rippled and splashed all
day long at the foot of the sloping ground
on which the house was built, and was
the source of endless fun and adventure.
Boating, bathing, fishing, and hunting for
crawfish in their hiding places under the
stones, were never-failing amusements
in summer; and when the bright waters
were ice-bound, his skates and his sledge
were in constant requisition. At the
time our story begins, the ice had just
broken up, and this year it had been
unusually grand. The great blocks up-

heaved with loud explosions, and groaned and creaked as they were jammed together into huge masses near the bridge, which was partially torn away and carried down the stream by the tremendous force of the pressure. It was a magnificent sight, though the damage caused by the floating ice was very great.

In a little cottage just across the river lived Philip Quin, with his widowed mother. He was Harry's school-fellow and inseparable companion. He was a pale, delicate boy, with brown hair and dark blue eyes; sensitive and shy in disposition, and very prone to spend more time over his books than his weakly constitution would allow. Harry, on the contrary, was fair-haired, tall, and robust; but he was not so studiously inclined as to be in any danger of impairing his health. The two boys were certainly very different, but such firm

friends that one seemed scarcely happy
without the other. Let us now follow
them down to the bridge, where they
are busy picking up the bits of wood old
Michael Lockyer casts aside in his work
of repair.

"I say, Mike," said Harry, "tell us
what this place was like when you first
came to live here."

The old man looked up. "Aye, Master Lynton, I've nigh forgot what them
days wor like, by now; but one thing I
know, it wasn't like it is at the present,
hereaway. Why, the woods came down
thick to the water's edge, and ne'er a
house nor yet a shanty stood up there
where Lyntonville is now; and yet that's
old, as we count it, for it's a matter o'
fifty year since the first log was laid."

"I suppose there were lots of wolves
and bears about here then," said Harry.
"You must have had many a brush with

them in your time, Mike. Tell us about
one, like a good old fellow; now do, I
know you can."

"Or about the beavers," interposed
Philip.

"Yes, yes, the beavers. Oh do,
Mike. I've heard you say before you
had seen them."

"Well, well, lads, I'll tell ye what I
can; but ye must let me get on with my
work, or I sha'n't be done by nightfall.
What was it I was going to tell ye?
Ah, the beavers, so it was. I do n't
know as how I ever had much to do with
'em, though. Do ye see that 'ere stump
down there? Well, that were some o'
their doin's."

"What, the beavers'?" exclaimed
Philip. "Why, they never could have
cut off such a tree as that."

"Aye, but they could though; and
those marks are nothing more nor less

than the nibbles o' their sharp teeth, I
can tell ye," said Mike.

"But did you ever see them?" asked
Harry.

"Why, yes, to be sure, many a time,
when I was a little chap. I used to come
about here with my father when he went
hunting. It's sixty year agone or more
since I first set eyes on that 'ere beaver
lodge, and now there a'n't so much as a
stick left. We lived a good bit away
then, so 't was a long trudge, and right
glad was I to hear the noise of the fall
down yonder. By and by my father
says to me, 'Now, Mike, you stand behind this tree and keep quiet, or you
wont have a chance to see 'em.' Well, I
looked, and there was the river dammed
up into a kind of pond like, with stakes
driven into the water, and wattled with
twigs like hurdles, and the holes filled in
with clay to make all tight, and round

the edge were ten or a dozen queer-look-
ing mud huts, but ne'er a beaver did I
see. 'Father,' says I, 'where are they?'
''Bide still,' says he, 'or you'll see
naught.' So I watched, and after a bit
a brown head popped up and looked all
around, and down he went again. Then
four or five came out of the huts, and
seemed to listen; and presently one of
'em gave a slap with his big flat tail, and
they all set to work mending a bit of the
dam that was broken down."

"Oh, Mike, I can't believe it," cried
Harry.

"Aye, but they did though," said
Mike, "and it was wonderful surely to
see 'em. If they'd been masons they
could n't ha' done their work better; and
how I did laugh to myself, to be sure, to
see one of 'em carrying the mortar on
his tail, and plasterin' up the wall as if
he'd been all his life a 'prentice to the

trade. There was one big fellow who seemed to be 'boss,' for whenever he slapped his tail, some of 'em went to do his bidding. After we 'd stood and looked at 'em a while, my father says to me, 'Now, Mike, we 'll go home; and do n't you forget the beavers, for there 's many a lesson you may learn from 'em.' 'No, father,' says I, 'for I shall know now what you mean when you say, 'as busy as a beaver.'' There 's none of 'em left now," added the old man as he took up his axe again, "for even then the trappers had found 'em out, and took a good many every year, for the sake of théir pelt and their tails, which are reckoned very good eating; and after a while the rest took fright, and forsook the dam."

" I 'll tell you what," said Harry, "I 'll ask papa to tell us more about them; and perhaps some day he may take us up the river far enough to find a beaver dam."

"I guess you'd have to go a goodish number of miles afore you came across one then," said Mike; "but it's getting late, and it's time for me to leave work, and so, my lads, I'll wish you a very good night."*

* It may be here observed that the beaver and the maple-leaf are the national emblems of the Canadas, and none more suitable could have been chosen; for the beaver speaks of unwearied diligence, while the maple-leaf represents the vast sources of wealth which the country affords, the maple being one of the most valuable of North American trees.

CHAPTER II.

THE LONG CROSS SCHOOL.

"From the neighboring school come the boys,
With more than their wonted noise
And commotion."

ABOUT two miles and a half from Lyntonville was the small village of Fairfield, consisting chiefly of one principal
street, which led straight across the
bridge and up the high bank of the river;
while two rival mills and a few frame
houses and shanties, dotted here and
there on the opposite side, comprised the
whole of the settlement. Standing a
short distance back from the top of the
steep village street was the little wooden
church. It was surrounded by a dark
background of pine-trees, which rocked
and swayed in the breeze, close by the
quiet churchyard, where many a settler

from the surrounding country had already
been laid to rest. Still further away to
the right, was the Long Cross school—a
low, rough building, with shingled roof,
and wooden walls grown grey by long
exposure to wind and weather. It de-
rived its name from being situated on
the Cross-road, leading through a large
cedar swamp, which connected the woods
of Lyntonville with those of Fairfield.
Had you peeped in at the door, you
would have seen boys of all sorts and
sizes, rich and poor, at the Long Cross
school, for there was no other for many
miles round. John and Charlie Redfern, the clergyman's sons, Tom Hardy
from the drygoods store at the corner,
and Philip Quin were all in the same
class with Harry Lynton and several
others; and we shall become better acquainted with some of them before our
story is finished.

One fine spring morning, Harry was walking leisurely to school, swinging his books by the leathern strap that bound them, when his quick eye spied a flying-squirrel, leaping from bough to bough in a large rock-elm close to the path. Immediately he gave chase, and after a long and exciting scramble, which led him far out of his road, he succeeded in securing it under his cap; and then he hurried on, eager to show his prize to his school-fellows. What was his dismay when he found the door closed, and heard through the open window the busy hum of the boys' voices repeating their lessons. There was no help for it now however, so he tried to slip in quietly unobserved. A class was just going up, and Harry thought he had escaped notice; but unfortunately it was by no means the first offence.

"I say, wont you catch it for being

late again," whispered his next neighbor. "Old Elmslie has been asking for you."

"Can't be helped," said Harry. "I've caught a flying-squirrel."

"Oh, do let us see it, Lynton," said Charlie Redfern; "where is it?"

"It's in my pocket; I can't show it to you now. It will be off, if I don't take care."

"I say, what's the fun?" telegraphed another from an opposite form. Harry drew a rough sketch on his slate and held it up.

"Silence, there," cried Mr. Elmslie from his desk, and instantly the boys were as still as mice. But Harry could think of nothing but his squirrel, which was bobbing about in his pocket, as if it would break bounds every moment. Soon the fifth form was called up; but not one word of his lesson could Harry remember, for the squirrel was still uppermost in his mind. "I say, Phil, do you think it will eat it's way out?" he whispered.

"What?" said Philip, who knew nothing about it.

"I've got a flying-squirrel in my pocket. I caught it coming to school."

"You'd better not bother about it now, you'll lose your place if you don't mind."

"Lynton," said the master, "you know the rules; go to the foot of the class, and don't let me have to speak to you again."

Harry tried to attend for a few minutes; then it struck him that the squirrel had been very still for a long time; could it be dead? He could not resist the temptation of putting his hand very gently into his pocket to see if all was right. Hardly had he done so, when a bite, sharp enough to draw blood, made him hastily withdraw it, and the little prisoner, taking advantage of the opening, sprang out of his pocket, and leaped first on the master's desk, where it upset the ink on his books and papers; then settled on little Percy Hamilton's curly head, entangling its claws in his long hair; then freeing itself with a struggle and a bound, it cleared the open window, and was off to the shelter of its native woods, well pleased no doubt to be let out of school. The boys shouted; those who were in the secret laughing heartily at poor Harry's misfortune, while the others, completely mystified at the sudden commotion, asked each other what it all meant. Even Mr. Elmslie's voice failed in quieting them for some moments; but order being at length restored, Harry was told to stand out.

"Now, sir," said the master, "what

am I to say to you for causing all this damage and disturbance?"

Harry stood silent, and the matter ended by his having to spend that long bright half-holiday alone in the Long Cross school, with all his lessons to learn over again.

But although Harry was inclined to be idle sometimes, he had nevertheless many good points in his character.   He was open-hearted and generous; and in any case of oppression or wrong-doing among his school-fellows, he was sure to stand up for the right.

It so happened that when Philip Quin first joined the school, he incurred the dislike of Tom Hardy, one of the biggest and most unpopular of the boys.   For a long time, Hardy, who was not wanting in quickness and ability, had been considered head of the fifth, or highest form; but he took advantage of his standing to

bully his companions. Very soon after
Philip joined however, Hardy found his
position becoming more and more unten-
able every day, and before many weeks
had passed he was completely outdone.
In consequence, Hardy lost no opportunity of annoying and holding him up to
ridicule, on the score of his poverty,
which was only too plainly betrayed by
his patched and threadbare coat. One
day Hardy was more than usually coarse
and rude in his conduct to Philip in the
playground, who bore it very meekly,
though his pale face glowed with the bright
flush of suppressed feeling. Presently
Harry was attracted by the loud tones of
Hardy's voice, and though he did not
know much of Philip at that time he could
not calmly see the weak oppressed.

"Come now, Hardy, you just stop that,
will you," said he ; "I'm not going to
stand it."

"Then just take yourself off, and leave me to mind my own business," said Hardy. "If you do n't look out I 'll pitch into you, my boy."

Some of the lads burst out laughing at this speech, for they all knew that Hardy's words were much more valiant than his deeds.

"Come on then," said Harry, "let's have it out, for you sha'n't bother Quin any more if I can help it."

"Oh do n't, Lynton, pray do n't fight on my account; what he says does me no harm, and I do n't mind ; please do n't ;" and Philip looked distressed. By this time however, Harry's coat was off, and a ring of boys had gathered around the combatants; most of them rallying round Harry, though one or two sided with his opponent. Hardy, like most bullies, was a sad coward, and he was rather frightened when he saw the turn affairs had taken; but he felt that if he showed the white feather now, he would lose his position in the playground as well as in his class, so with a great deal of bluster he prepared to fight his young antagonist. Several blows were struck on both sides, and Harry succeeded in punishing Hardy severely, though a bruised face and black eye proved that he himself had not escaped in defending the weak. At this moment Mr. Elmslie rather unexpectedly made his appearance.

. "Now, boys, what's all this about?" said he very gravely. "Go, Lynton, and wash your face, and then come into school, where I will speak to you, which I cannot do in your present state." Harry walked off, looking very deplorable.

"Who was the other?" continued Mr. Elmslie, looking round, but Hardy had contrived to slip off unobserved, and was not to be seen.

"If you please, sir," said Philip, coming forward and speaking very earnestly, "do n't blame Lynton, for he did it out of kindness; indeed he did, sir, though I begged him not."

" A strange way of showing kindness, truly. And are you mixed up in this affair too, Quin? I should not have believed it possible," said Mr. Elmslie, in evident displeasure.

Philip colored, and did not know what to say, for he could not bear to have his friend suffer unjustly, while he did not like to allude to Hardy's provoking and unkind taunts about his poverty. He stood silent for a moment, and then said, very respectfully, "If you please, sir, may I explain? Hardy was teasing me, and Harry took my part, which led to the fight."

" There seems to have been very small provocation, Quin; and as I entirely disapprove of the practice, I shall certainly make examples of Lynton and Hardy."

"Oh, sir," cried Charlie Redfern, a bright little fellow of eleven, who was never afraid of speaking his mind; "Oh, Mr. Elmslie, it would n't be fair, indeed it would n't. Hardy is a big bully, and he is always going on at Quin about being poor, and I do n't know what all. It's more than any fellow can stand, sir; and it's all because he gets above him in school. It's a downright shame the way he goes on, and Lynton said he would n't stand it any longer, for Quin bears it so meekly and never says a word. It's Hardy that's to blame if any one is; you would have thought so yourself, sir, if you had been here." And he stopped, breathless with his long speech.

"Is this the case, boys?"

"Yes, sir." "It is really, sir," cried several voices together.

"Well, then," said Mr. Elmslie as Harry reappeared, "that alters the case. I am glad to find, Lynton, that you are not so much to blame in this matter as I imagined at first; but, boys, I wish I could teach you to remember that this is not the way to settle disputes, or make wrong come right. I am very thankful, Quin, to find that you do not harbor ill-will, or desire to resent an injury. I trust the disposition to bear meekly with insults proceeds from a truly noble effort on your part, my boy," and Mr. Elmslie looked kindly at Philip; "I mean an effort to follow in the steps of Him who was meek and lowly in heart, and forgave every trespass. As for Hardy, he must be differently dealt with."

CHAPTER III.

SIGHTS IN THE WOOD.

"There's not a leaf within the bower,
There's not a bird upon the tree,
There's not a dew-drop on the flower,
But bears the impress, Lord, of thee.
Yes, dew-drops, leaves, and birds, and all
The smallest like the greatest things,
The sea's vast space, the earth's wide ball,
Alike proclaim thee King of kings."

FROM the day of the fight, Harry and Philip had been fast friends, and many a pleasant expedition they had together. Harry's open, fearless character had a good influence upon Philip, who was timid and sensitive; while Philip's high principles and thoughtful piety were a check upon Harry's natural heedlessness. One Saturday, being a holiday, Harry ran off as usual to seek his friend; and when he reached the cottage, he found him sitting in an arbor in the garden reading.   This little retreat was the work of Philip's own hands, and he had spent many busy hours in its construction.   He could even tell the spot where each knotted stick and fir-cone and curious pebble had been found.   When at length the last nail was driven in, and he had really completed his long-cherished design, his delight was great, and he was proud indeed when his mother promised to honor his little edifice by drinking tea there with him the first evening after it was finished.   Harry's emulation had been roused by the successful labors of his companion, and he too had attempted something of the same kind; but he soon became weary of his work, and gave it up, like many other things which he had thrown aside in the same way.

Philip looked up as Harry's shadow fell on his open book.

"Oh, Harry," said he, "are you going for a walk?"

"Yes," cried Harry, "come along; it's so jolly in the woods to-day, and we shall find ever so many thinge."

Philip went in to tell his mother, and then joined his friend, and the two lads set off together. The woods certainly were very inviting, for flowers of every hue sprang up at their feet, and every little hillock was carpeted with soft mosses and crowned with the delicate fronds of the oak-fern or the glossy black stems of the maiden-hair. Large lily-like plants, called by the Indians "deaths," on account of the deadly poison which lurks beneath their fair appearance, nodded their beautiful snowy or chocolate-colored blossoms in the breeze. The sunlight shimmered and glanced through the waving boughs, brightening the little nooks and dells, here flecking the sober

pines with its golden gleam, there kiss-
ing the ripe red strawberries scattered
in abundance over the ground.   But
amid all these beauties Philip looked
grave and out of spirits; and at length
he said, "It was this day three years
ago that my father died."

"Do you remember him?" asked
Harry.

"Oh, yes, quite well.   I was ten then,
and we had just come over from Ireland,
mamma, and papa, and Edith—that was
my little sister—and our old nurse Norah.   I remember so well, the day we
arrived at Montreal, seeing the squaws
come on board ship with their baskets
and moccasins for sale.   I was frightened rather, and so was Edie, until mamma told us all about them.   Well, we
staid there some time, and then papa
heard of a farm that would suit him, and
it was while we were on our journey to

the place, I forget the name, that papa was taken ill of cholera and died. Then Edie took it, and old Norah, and they were all buried in the same grave."

"Oh Philip; how dreadful."

"Yes," said Philip, "it was a dreadful time. And afterwards mamma was very ill; and when she got better we came here. I remember Edie and I had ponies in the old country, and we used to ride with papa very often. I never had a shabby coat then;" and Philip looked down at his well-worn sleeves, patched in more than one place; "but that does n't matter," he added hastily, "it 's mamma that I care about. If I were only a man, I could earn something to make her more comfortable."

"Well," said Harry, "you are so smart that you will be able to do it some day. It 's my belief you could teach a school as well as Mr. Elmslie now."

Thus chatting together, Philip became more cheerful, and the two boys kept along the edge of the forest for some distance, gathering the strawberries, and filling their hands with the different wild flowers that tempted them on at every step.

"I say, look here," said Harry, "the mandrakes are out;" and he lifted one of the broad twin-leaves of a curious-looking plant, and showed Philip a large white waxen flower, like a wild rose, growing close to the foot-stalk, which had been hidden from sight. "We must mark the place, and come here when the fruit is ripe."

"What is it like?" said Philip.

"It is about the size of an egg, and has a thick yellow skin, with seeds like a gooseberry. It's first-rate, I can tell you. Suppose we go further into the wood now, we sha'n't find much more out here."

"What's this?" said Philip as he stooped to pick up something that looked like a tobacco-pipe curiously carved in wax, stuck into the ground bowl upwards, at the foot of a pine.

"Oh, I'm so glad you've found one," cried Harry; "it must be the 'Indian pipe' old Mike told me about. I believe it's nothing but a fungus; see, it's turning black already. Did n't it look just as if some one had put it there and forgotten it?"

"Oh, did you see that bird?" exclaimed Philip abruptly; "it was bright scarlet, and passed like a flash of fire."

"It's a tannager; but it is not all scarlet; it has black wings, I know, because papa has one stuffed. Yes, there he goes; and there's a blue jay. Hark! do you hear his scream?"

And so, attracted by one strange sight after another, the boys wandered on decper and deeper into the forest, until at last Philip said, "Do n't you think we ought to be going home, Harry? It must be getting late."

They had left the little wood-path a long while before, to pick a flower here and to get a glimpse of a squirrel or bright bird there; and now, when it was time for them to retrace their steps, they could not remember in which direction they had come. Above and around them were thick tall trees, so tall that they could only catch a glimpse of the sky now and then, and not a sign of a footpath could they see. Their feet sank deep into the rich soft mould formed by the fallen leaves for hundreds of years, and it seemed as if no other footstep had ever passed that way. The two boys stood still for a moment and consulted.

"Here 's a pretty go," said Harry;

"I'm sure I do n't remember which way
we came; do you?"

"No," said Philip, looking very much
frightened; "the trees are all alike, and
there's no path. What shall we do,
Harry?"

"Oh, never mind; we'll soon find it.
I think it was this way; we'll try it, at
any rate."

They turned in the direction he indi-
cated, and walked on for some distance
without speaking.

"Do you remember that fallen tree,
Harry?" said Quin as they came to a
large trunk completely uprooted, lying
all across their path.

"I can't say I do, Philip. I'm afraid
we're wrong, after all; we must go back."

Again they turned, and as they went
the undergrowth seemed to become thick-
er as it brushed past their faces and
scratched and tore their clothes, which

made them think they were going farther and farther into the wood. Up and
down they wandered, Harry saying all
he could think of to keep up poor Phil-.
ip's courage, though it must be confessed
his own was fast oozing away, for the
time was passing on. It was getting
dark, as the sun had nearly set. They
felt that the blackness of night would
soon be upon them, and they were alone
in the great silent forest. Philip held
Harry's hand tightly clasped in his own,
and they looked at each other without
speaking a word. Just then a large bird
flew up, and startled them with its heavy
flight, and all was still again; so still that
they could almost hear their hearts beat-
ing.

"Oh, Harry," said Philip at last,
"what will my mother do when she finds
we do n't come back? Do you think we
shall ever find our way back?"

"I do n't know," said Harry; "perhaps they 'll look for us; but I 'm afraid they do n't know which way we went. I wonder if any one would hear, if we shouted?"

Again and again they shouted, but the sound only waked the echoes of the forest, and startled one or two birds that had gone to roost in the trees near; so they gave it up in despair.

Presently Harry said, "Philip, let us kneel down and pray; perhaps God will help us."

They knelt down hand in hand at the foot of a tree, and Philip uttered a few words of earnest prayer that God would take care of them, and bring them back safely to their homes. When they rose from their knees Philip said, "Do you remember the psalm, Harry, 'Thou compassest my path and my lying down, and art acquainted with all my ways. The

night shineth as the day: the darkness
and the light are both alike to thee?' I
do n't think we ought to be afraid, for
God is with us here just as much as if
we were at home."

"But, Philip, suppose we are starved
to death!"

"Oh but, Harry, we 've asked God to
take care of us; and I know he will, because he has promised to hear our prayers for Christ's sake."

The two boys began to feel more hope-
ful as, comforting each other, they thus
remembered that their Father in heaven
was near, however far they might be
from their earthly parents' aid.

CHAPTER IV.

A NIGHT IN THE FOREST.

"Abide with me ; fast falls the eventide,
The darkness thickens ; Lord, with me abide.
When other helpers fail, and comforts flee,
Help of the helpless, Oh, abide with me."

"I wish we could light a fire, Harry ; it's getting very dark, and. I 'm so cold."

"Ah, that's a capital idea, and I believe we can do it too, for I 've got the matches in my pocket that we were going to use when we fired off the cannon yesterday."

They set to work and gathered a large heap of dry wood, which after many failures they managed to light with some dead leaves, and soon it burned up brightly. The fire was a great comfort, and afforded them some occupation, for

they employed all the little light that
was left in making a pile of sticks to
keep it up all night. This done, they
sat down by it, and tried to make themselves as comfortable as they could under the circumstances. It was now quite
dark, and they talked as much as possible, for the dead silence was more than
they could bear. Now and then the dry
wood crackled and flared up, and as soon
as the flame died away they piled on
more fuel to keep up a blaze. Sleep of
course was out of the question, and they
sat there listening to every little sound,
and conjuring up all sorts of terrors, both
real and imaginary. The rustle of a
dead leaf was enough to make them start;
and once, when a wild, unearthly scream
broke the stillness of the night, just above
their heads, they clung to each other in
terrible fear, until they heard the heavy
flapping of wings, and remembered it

could be nothing but an owl in search of its prey.

Slowly and wearily passed the time; each moment seemed an hour to their excited fancy; but as the night wore on they became more calm, and Harry had nearly regained his wonted courage, when they heard a heavy, crashing sound, as of some large animal coming through the brushwood. Nearer and nearer it approached, and their hearts died within them; they hardly dared to breathe, lest the sound should attract the attention of the beast. They each caught up a lighted brand from the fire as the only weapon within reach, and put themselves in an attitude of defence. Presently the bushes on the other side of the fire parted; they saw two red eyeballs glaring at them, and could just distinguish the huge outlines of a bear through the gloom. There it stood for some time,

evidently not knowing what to make of
the unwonted sight of a fiery pile in its
hitherto undisturbed haunts; and there
stood the boys, motionless, their eyes
fixed on the unwelcome invader of their
solitude. After a while it gave a low
growl, and raising its head, snuffed about
as if in search of them; but at that moment the fire, which was getting low, fell
in, and a bright blaze shot up, crackling
and sparkling as it rose. This seemed
to alarm the bear, which is well known
to be a cowardly animal, unless suffering
from extreme hunger. It turned with a
parting grunt, and slowly trotted off,
and they heard its retreating footsteps
growing fainter and more faint in the
distance. After this they had no further
alarms, but the time seemed to pass more
tediously than ever, for they feared lest
their dreaded enemy should return again.
Most thankful were they when the first

pale streaks of dawning light told them
that morning was near, and that the long
horrible darkness was past.

"It's Sunday morning, Philip," said
Harry.

"Yes," whispered Philip, "we ought
to thank God;" and once again they
knelt to render their heartfelt praise for
their preservation from the dangers of the
night.

At length, when it was light enough
for them to see each other distinctly,
Harry was startled to observe how haggard poor Philip looked. He was not a
strong boy at any time, and want of food
for so many hours, combined with the
terrors of their situation, had been too
much for him; but he said nothing, and
they began to look about for wild berries to satisfy their hunger. They could
find nothing, however, but a few plants
of the Indian turnip.

"Do you know, Philip," said Harry, "I 've heard that the Indians eat these roots; but if they are not cooked in one particular way, they hurt one's throat and mouth most fearfully. I believe they roast them. Shall we try? We shall starve if we do n't eat something, and there are no berries about here."

"Yes, perhaps it would be a good plan," said Philip, "but I can't say I feel very hungry."

Harry pulled up some of the roots and washed them in a little stream hard by; then covering them with the hot wood embers, he piled on more sticks, and left them to roast themselves. "What had we better do?" said he; "shall we try again to find our way back? If we could only get to the river, we should be all right. You know we could notch the trees, so that we might find the fire again."

Philip agreed to this proposal, but Harry was shocked to see him sink back faint as he tried to rise.

"Oh, Philip, dear Philip, what is the matter? What shall I do if you are ill? Stay, I 'll get some water;" and hurrying down to the tiny stream, he soon came back with some in his cap, and kneeling down he began to bathe Philip's face. It was some time before he opened his eyes.

"There, that's right, old fellow; you'.. be better directly. It 's because we have not eaten any thing for so long," said Harry. "I feel very queer too. But how cold you are;" and in a moment his coat was off, and he was wrapping it round his friend.

"Hark! I heard a shout; I am certain I did," cried he joyfully. They listened intently, and again the welcome sound broke upon their ears. Harry shouted

with all his might; and then, to their
intense joy, they heard footsteps ap-
proaching, and presently the friendly
dusky face of old Peter Muskrat, an Indian well known in the neighborhood,
appeared through the trees.   Over his
shoulder was slung a fawn, and the string
of black bass in his hand showed he had
been on a foraging expedition.   Indeed
so good a hunter was he, that Mr. Lynton was accustomed to take him as a
guide in his autumn hunting excursions.
The boys made him understand that they
had lost their way, and asked him to help
them.

    "Ugh!   Lynton good man," said he;
"take boys home—give Peter blanket-
coat for winter.   Come—squaw give
food—wigwam not far off."   Then seeing
Philip looked pale and weak, he pro-
duced a flask from a sort of birch-bark
knapsack, and made him swallow a

mouthful of something which took away his breath, and proved to be whisky. It revived him, however; but as he still lagged behind, old Peter took him up in his strong arms and carried him, while Harry followed with some of the Indian's spoils. After a while they began to hear the roar of the river, and a turn in the path brought them in sight of the Indian camp.

It consisted of a few tent-like wigwams, and at the doors, or rather entrances of two or three of them, sat several squaws, some making baskets to sell in the neighboring villages, and others engaged in ornamenting their deerskin moccasins with bright-colored beads. They all wore the embroidered leggings and moccasins of their tribe, but the rest of their costume was a motley mixture of civilized attire and their own native garments. One old squaw, who proved to

be Muskrat's wife, was watching a huge
pot, hung over a wood fire by means of
stakes driven into the ground, the contents of which she stirred now and then
with a stick.   Old Peter threw down the
fawn and the fish at the door of his wigwam, and speaking to his wife in their
own language, they conferred together
for some minutes.   The boys could not
help laughing at some of the little baby
Indians—papooses as they called them—
which were bound in tight swathing bands
to a flat piece of birch-bark, and were
hung up in any available situation,
whence they peered about with their
round black eyes.   "They are just like
the tails of Bo-peep's sheep," said Harry,
"all hung on a tree to dry."   By this
time several more men made their appearance, but took very little notice of
the boys beyond the customary "ugh"
and a shrug of their broad shoulders.

Presently the old squaw turning out the contents of the great pot into a sort of wooden bowl or platter, they gathered round it, helping themselves with their fingers, while the women kept at a respectful distance. Peter gave the two boys some of this savory dish in a smaller bowl, and though they wondered what they were eating, they were too hungry to be very fastidious, and Harry at least did ample justice to the meal. "I shouldn't be surprised if this were bull-frog stew," said he to Philip; "I know these fellows eat them, and the little bones look very suspicious. However, I sha'n't ask any questions; I never was so hungry in all my life."

"I wonder whether they will show us the way home soon," said Philip, who seemed more anxious for that than for any thing else, "and whether any one has been looking for us." By this time they had finished, and old Muskrat brought them the bottle, which had been passing pretty freely from mouth to mouth, but the boys shook their heads. "No!" said he in surprise; "leetle boys not know what's good;" then putting it to his own mouth, he drank off their share as if it were so much water.

"Peter's squaw show way—Lynton give blanket-coat," said he as the old woman came out of her wigwam, baskets in hand, in hopes of getting customers at Lyntonville. "Yes, yes," said Harry, much amused at his anxiety to be paid for his trouble. Taking a penknife, which happened to be nearly new, out of his pocket, he gave it to the old man, who grinned with delight. They then bade adieu to the friendly Indians, and with a last look at the funny little papooses, they followed the Indian along the banks of the river, and were amazed to find how

soon they reached their own familiar
haunts.

When they came in sight of the house,
Harry threw up his cap and shouted
"hurrah" at the top of his voice. The
two mothers, who were together, heard
the welcome sound, and hardly daring
to believe that their ears had not deceived them, rushed into the verandah,
and in a few moments the boys were
clasped in their arms. "My dear, dear
boys," said Mrs. Lynton; "thank God,
we have you safe again. Where have
you been? Your father, Harry, and
the neighbors have been out all night
searching for you."

Numberless were the questions that
poured in upon them; and meanwhile
the old squaw stood with characteristic
patience awaiting their leisure, for she
had no idea of departing without a gift
of some sort. She was liberally reward-

ed, and obtained a promise of the blanket-coat upon which old Peter seemed to have set his heart. A meal was also provided for her, and to the boys' astonishment, she not only managed to dispose of a large portion of a round of beef, but stowed away the remainder in her basket, as well as the rest of a loaf of goodly size which had been placed before her. The boys were not aware that Indian etiquette obliged her to do this, as to leave any food put before them on the table would be considered a breach of good manners.

CHAPTER V.

BREAKING-UP DAY AT SCHOOL.

" 'T is not the eye of keenest blaze,
Nor the quick-swelling breast,
That soonest thrills at touch of praise :
These do not please Him best."

IT was too late to attend the morning
service, which must have been already
begun ere they reached their home, and
the boys were glad to rest a while after
their long walk and sleepless night; but
in the afternoon the whole party set out
for the little church at Fairfield. As
they approached, the bell began to ring,
and Philip thought he had never heard
music so sweet as that which called the
worshippers together to the house of God.
They entered the church with hearts
thankful that they were once more per-

mitted to engage all together in the service of the sanctuary. Earnestly they joined in the prayers and praises which were offered; and when Mr. Redfern the minister went into the pulpit and gave out his text, Harry and Philip were struck with the singular appropriateness of the passage. It was this: "Oh that men would praise the Lord for his goodness, and for his wonderful works to the children of men!" Psa. 107 : 8. They listened still more attentively when the preacher referred to the verses preceding it: "They wandered in the wilderness in a solitary way; they found no city to dwell in. Hungry and thirsty, their soul fainted in them. Then they cried unto the Lord in their trouble, and he delivered them out of their distresses. And he led them forth by the right way, that they might go to a city of habitation."

"My brethren," said the good man, "who is there among us that cannot testify to the goodness of the Lord? Who cannot point to some special deliverance at some time or other of their lives— some danger averted, or life spared, when no human arm was near to aid, no human voice to comfort and assure? Aye, and when the cry for help and deliverance from the threatened danger has been wrung from a full heart, has it not many a time been coupled with a vow, that once free, once escaped, the spared life should be devoted to the service of the strong Deliverer? If any such are here, let me urge them to remember that hour, and to pay unto the Lord these solemn vows.

"But while we consider these verses in their literal meaning, we must not forget that there are far greater perils besetting each precious soul, than any that can happen to the body. My friends, have we not all wandered from the strait path? Have we not all strayed into the wilderness of this sinful world, and turned aside from the narrow gate which leadeth unto life? The pleasures of sin have lured us on and on, like the bright flowers by the wayside, until at length our feet begin to stumble upon the slippery paths, and thorns and briers grow up where the fragrant blossoms have been. What a picture is here of the world which lieth in wickedness. Thanks be to God, some among us have escaped from its snares, and can now join in the song of the redeemed. But are there none here whose souls are fainting within them because the pleasures have faded, and the troubles and the weariness of sin remain? Oh, my brethren, there is redemption for *you;* there is a city to dwell in prepared for *you;* if you will only seek it in the

right way, through the blood and right
eousness of our loving Saviour. In Christ
there is deliverance; in Christ there is
rest; in Christ there is pardon and peace.
He is the Door—we must enter by him.
He is the Way—we must follow him.
He is the Rock—we must trust in him.
He is the Life—in him we have life everlasting.

"Let us ask the aid of his promised
Comforter, the Holy Spirit, to teach us all
things and testify to us of him; to work
in us the grace of true repentance; to
guide us into all truth, and deliver us
from all evil. Without the help of the
Holy Spirit we can do nothing; but we
never seek his aid in vain, for our Lord
himself has said, 'If ye then, being evil,
know how to give good gifts unto your
children, how much more shall your
heavenly Father give the Holy Spirit to
them that ask him.' Luke 11:13.

"Thus, trusting in Christ alone, and relying on the promised help of his Holy Spirit, we shall be enabled to praise the Lord, not only with our lips but in our lives, walking before him in 'holiness and righteousness all the days of our life.'"

As the boys walked home together after service, Harry looked very grave, and was silent for some time. At length he said, "Oh, Philip, did not the sermon seem like a message to us? I am sure we ought to praise God for being saved from death. When the bear came so close to us last night, I prayed to God to deliver us; and I thought if we could only get safe home again, I would serve God all my life. But, Philip, it is so hard for us boys to do any thing to serve God: if we were men it would be a different thing. I do n't see what I can do 'to show forth his praise.'"

'I do n't know," said Philip; "but it seems to me that all we can do is to try and do our best in our every day duties, I .mean our lessons and things; because I have heard my mother say that God has a work for every one to do, according to his age and station in life. You remember that verse where St. Paul says, 'With good will doing service, as to the Lord, and not to men;' and do n't you think we can serve God by being steady and diligent and obedient, and all that?"

"I suppose that is the way, Phil; but I always forget."

"We must ask God to help us, Harry, by his Holy Spirit, for Christ's sake," said Philip.

Philip's advice was remembered, and from this time Harry did become m industrious and painstaking; and his mother's heart rejoiced when she saw her son striving to do his duty for the Lord's sake.

The two boys were the heroes of the school on the following day, and they had to relate their adventures again and again for the amusement of their companions. The Wednesday after this event had been fixed for the examination and breaking up of the school for the summer vacation. As many parents came on that day to assure themselves of their sons' progress during the past term, the boys always endeavored to make their school look as festive as possible, by decking it with cedar-boughs and bright flowers. The examination this year was more largely attended than usual; and Mrs. Lynton persuaded Mrs. Quin to join their party, as it was understood that Philip would be declared first in the school. Some of the parents had subscribed a sum sufficient to enable Mr. Elmslie to give a few

prizes for the encouragement of his schol-
ars, though it was not the usual custom
of the school. Great was the excitement
therefore on the appointed day, for
none of the boys knew who would be the
fortunate winners of the much-coveted
prizes.

The examination was to begin at two
o'clock, and before that hour many visit-
ors had arrived. The younger boys, for
Mr. Elmslie began with the lower class-
es, acquitted themselves very fairly, and
received a general commendation for diligence in their studies.

At length it was the turn of the first
class to go up, and greater interest began
to be shown, as it was to be subjected to a
much more difficult examination. Philip,
though evidently nervous, passed most
creditably, and without a doubt was entitled to hold the first place. Harry,
much to his own surprise, ranked second.

Poor Hardy, who had hitherto looked upon the examination as his own particular triumph, was completely crestfallen that he was so far down on the list. Philip therefore received the prize for general proficiency in school work; and as each class was only entitled to one prize, the others were distributed among the younger boys.

When all were given, it was seen that Mr. Elmslie laid a handsomely bound Bible upon the desk before him, and addressing the boys, he said, "My lads, it has given me much pleasure to distribute among you the prizes which have been kindly placed at my disposal to bestow upon those who deserve encouragement for diligent attention to their studies. Of course, where there are so many competitors, it must necessarily happen that many are disappointed. To these I would say one cheering word; that while *one* in each class has done best, yet there are several who have done well. It is not always the boy who works hardest that wins the prize; for ability and quickness go far to help some, of whose industry I cannot say much. I have therefore made out a list of those in the whole school, whom I find by my books to merit special commendation, which I have now much pleasure in reading."

Here followed a long list of names; and many a little boy's eyes sparkled with delight when he heard his own among them. Mr. Elmslie at length folded up the paper, and continued, "The prizes which have been bestowed among you to-day, are simply intended, as you all know, to testify to your proficiency in the various branches of study in which you are engaged. To the number of these I have added one as a reward for good conduct during the past year, and a token of my own regard for the boy who best deserves it. I have chosen a Bible for this purpose; first, because it is the best of all books; and secondly, because it is the best of all guides in enabling those who seek instruction from its pages to lead a God-fearing, useful, and noble life. I have endeavored to choose among you all as impartially as possible, and I hope when I name Philip Quin as the owner of the book I hold in my hand, that my choice will be approved by his companions."

"Hurrah, yes, yes. He is a good fellow," cried many voices; and Philip, with much surprise and a glowing face, went up to the desk to receive the beautiful gift.

"And now, my lads," resumed Mr. Elmslie, "I will not detain you longer than to wish you all a very pleasant holiday; and may God have us all in his most holy keeping, both now and always."

The boys began to cheer as soon as he had finished, and very soon the books were passing from hand to hand, exciting many remarks and great admiration. Philip found his way at once to his mother's side. Her eyes were full of tears as she whispered a few words of loving approval to her only son, who gave promise of being a real blessing and comfort to his widowed mother. Very soon the school-house was empty, and various groups of the boys and their parents were seen wending their way to their several homes; and very few carried away with them any other feelings than those of pleasure and satisfaction at the events of the day.

There was one however whose face wore a scowl as he met Philip, and in whose heart evil feelings of anger and

revenge were burning. This one was
Tom Hardy. Never before had an examination passed so much to his disad-
vantage, and his was not the disposition
to bear meekly any fancied wrong. Poor
boy, we must not judge him too harshly,
for he had few of the advantages our
young friends Harry and Philip possess-
ed. No loving mother had he, to soothe
his angry spirit or gently to instil holy
principles into his mind; and his father
was a harsh, money-making and money-
loving man, with little time and less in-
clination to train his children in a right
way.

Tom was reckoned a sharp, smart lad,
and Mr. Hardy's friends did not fail to
speak honied words of praise of him, too
often in his hearing, in order to curry
favor with his father, who was looked
upon by some of the smaller settlers as
a great man in that district. Tom Hardy

left the school-house with angry thoughts
in his heart and angry words on his lips.
"I'll be even with him yet," said he to
himself; "I thought something was in
the wind, with his meek religious ways,
sneak as he is, all to get on the right
side of old Elmslie; but I'll teach him."
He seemed lost in thought for a while,
and then quickening his pace, muttering
in a low tone, "That will do; I've hit it,"
he ran down the hill and disappeared.

But what was passing in Philip's mind
at the same time? We fear a humble,
lowly spirit was no longer his; for as he
passed Hardy his heart glowed with ex-
ultation at his own success, and his feelings were akin to those of the Pharisee
who dared to thank God that he was not
as other men. Ah, how short, at any
time, is the step between us and sin;
and what need to pray for God's pre-
venting grace. All day he hugged vain

thoughts of his goodness close to his heart, though none suspected it; but afterwards, when he knelt down at night, his conscience smote him as he remembered that his Father in heaven, from whom no secrets are hid, had read the thoughts of his inmost heart. A sense of his sin in God's sight weighed him down, and he whom all had praised that day closed it in the secrecy of his own little chamber with the heartfelt prayer, "God be merciful to me a sinner."

In the mean time the Lyntonville party, with the addition of Mrs. Quin, Philip, and Mr. Elmslie, had reached home, and the pleasant day was brought to a close by a row in Mr. Lynton's large boat on the river. The short twilight had already begun, but a bright star twinkled here and there in the dark blue sky, to light them on their way. There was a hush in the air which told of the coming hours of stillness and rest, broken only by the sighing of the wind in the tree-tops, mingled with the distant lowing of cattle or the loud croak of the bullfrog close at hand. Fireflies flitted about, gleaming like flashing emeralds among the low bushes by the water-side; and the plash of the oars kept time to the evening hymn begun by Mrs. Lynton's sweet voice, and sung in chorus by all the party. Harry thought he had never loved their beautiful river so much before; and he bade his friend "goodnight" with unmingled happiness, rejoicing in his success. The dew was falling fast, and the night wind blew with a chilly breath as they hastened homeward; but little did any of them dream of the change that a few short hours would work on that peaceful scene.

CHAPTER VI.

WHAT CAME OF IT.

"Fire is a good servant, but a bad master."
"Behold, how great a matter a little fire kindleth!"

HAD any one watched the stealthy footsteps of a boy who, under the darkening shades of that summer night, left the village of Fairfield and proceeded in the direction of Mrs. Quin's cottage, they could hardly have failed to suspect mischief; and Tom Hardy, for it was he, might well stop at every sound, and draw back into deeper shadow. It was but the wind however, as it blew back the hair from his hot forehead, or the echo of his own footfall in the stillness, that startled him. His conscience whispered, "Turn back, Tom, turn back; think what you are going to do;" but in vain; Tom

would not listen. He tried to stifle its
voice. "It was no such great matter,
after all " said he to himself; he was
only going to set fire to Philip's bower;
that would do him no real harm; he
might build it again, if he liked. It
would but make him angry; and then
what fun it would be to see Philip, the
meek. Philip, in a rage next morning,
when he found a few smouldering ruins
all that remained of his work. The best
of it would be too, that no one would be
able to discover the cause of the fire; he
would take good care of that. And
Hardy laughed a low, exultant laugh as
he thought over the capital revenge he
had planned.

By this time he had reached the house.
All was still, and he crept round to the
back, and looked up at the windows.
"There's no light," thought he, " so they
must be in bed and asleep." Stealing

to the arbor, he began carefully to build
up beside it a small stack of tarred sticks
and shavings just where the rising wind
would fan the flame, when the loud crow-
ing of a cock close by made him start
and listen ; but all was silent again, and
he went on with his work. When it was
done to his satisfaction, he struck a match ;
guarding it with trembling hands from
the breeze which threatened to put it out,
and stooping slowly, he applied the light
to the little heap. Then, only waiting
an instant to make sure that the shavings had caught fire, he fled away from
the spot as though he were pursued, and
never once looked behind him until he
reached the village. Creeping quietly
in by a back way, he managed to elude
observation, and watching his opportunity, got up to his room, and lay down
on his bed as he had done many a night
before, unnoticed by any of the house-

hold, a prayerless, ungodly, miserable
boy.

He could not sleep. Every sound
startled him ; and he wondered as he
lay in the dark whether Philip had been
awakened by the red glare of the burning summer-house or by the crackling of
the flames. The possibility had escaped
him before, but now it seemed unlikely
that they could sleep through it. Rest-
less and feverish with excitement, he
tossed about from one side to the other.
Then it struck him that the match might
have been blown out by a puff of wind
before it had time thoroughly to kindle
the shavings. There was relief in the
thought ; and as he flung off the light
bedclothes to cool his fevered limbs he
exclaimed, "I hope it is n't burning. I
shall be glad, after all, though I did want
to tease him." But the little pile of
sticks—that would lead to suspicion ; and

he would be suspected too, as his feelings towards Quin were well known. "Oh," he cried, "I wish I had n't done it; what a fool I have been." His teeth began to chatter, and he pulled the bedclothes up again. "Well, I must go the first thing in the morning, before it's light," thought he, "and take 'em away, if they have n't caught; and if I do meet any one about, I 'll tell 'em I 'm looking for a robin's nest or something. How the wind is rising too. What if it is burning, after all ?"

But hark! the boy sprang up, for the loud clang of the fire-bell broke upon his ear. His heart died within him; it was discovered. All Fairfield was speedily aroused. "Fire! fire!" shouted a voice in the street, and Tom heard his father open his window and ask in what direction it was.

"Can't quite make out," said the man;

"down by the river somewhere. May-
hap it's only a barn; but I'm off to see."
Then came the loud rattle of the engine
as the firemen dragged it down the village street; and Tom's door opened, and
his father called out, "Come on, Tom,
I'm going to see the fun; they say it's
the widow Quin's cottage." Tom pretended to wake from a deep sleep.
"What's the matter?" said he, as well
as his choking voice would let him.

"Why, it's a fire, lad, a fire. You
can't be sleeping through all this din,
surely. Come along with me; I'm going down."

"I don't care to see it," said Tom
gruffly; "I'm sleepy;" and he turned
over again as if in a heavy slumber.
Mr. Hardy hurried off.

The cottage on fire! Oh no, it could
not be; it was too terrible to be true.
Surely the cottage was too far off to be

in any danger. Tom shivered from head
to foot, and the perspiration streamed
down his face. He never dreamed that
it would come to this; and if it should
be discovered that he had lit that dreadful fire, what then? He would be thrown
into prison, and brought to trial before a
judge. Mingled with his terror of an
earthly tribunal came a vague recollec-
tion of words from God's book, of awful
woe to those who "devoured widows'
houses."

Eagerly he listened, straining his ear
to catch every distant sound, till he could
bear the suspense no longer, and hurrying on his clothes, he rushed out into the
street. He knew only too well the direction in which to go, and when he reached
the bridge he could see the lurid sky
and the fierce flames leaping up through
the thick smoke, though the cottage was
partly hidden by trees. It was too true,

and he covered his face with his hands
to shut out the terrible sight. "Oh,"
he exclaimed, "I did not mean to do any
thing so dreadful as this; I never thought
the fire would go further than the bower;
what shall I do? what shall I do?" But
it was useless to loiter, and he rushed
madly on. Once his foot caught in a
stump, and he fell heavily; but he was
up in a moment, and ran on again until
he reached the spot.

What a sight it was! The engine was
working, but not effectively, for part of
the machinery needed repair; and the
red flames shot up, hissing and roaring,
licking up the water with their forked
tongues, and destroying all before them.
Not a hope remained of saving any part
of the building. Tom saw Philip with
Harry Lynton and several other lads,
but he avoided them, and asked a fire-
man where Mrs. Quin was.

"They've taken her up to Lyntonville. It's a terrible business for her,
poor thing," said the man as he hurried
away.

The parlor as yet had not suffered
much, for the back of the house had
caught fire first; and it came into Tom's
mind to try and rescue something. He
forced his way into the room through the
scorching heat and smoke. Most of the
furniture had been removed; but a few
things still remained, and lying on a
chair was Philip's beautiful Bible and
his prize. Could it really be so short a
time since the books were placed in his
hands, and yet that they had become the
innocent cause of all this evil? Oh that
Tom could have recalled those hours; he
would not have acted as he had done.
He caught up the books, and as he
tried to pass out his foot struck against
something on the floor. It was a small

miniature portrait. He picked it up
and made his way to the door; but the
flames had burst into the passage and
drove him back, while a shout was raised
outside that the roof was falling. Not a
moment was to be lost, and he dashed
through the smoke and flame only just in
time to escape being crushed beneath the
falling rafters; as it was, his hair and
clothes were singed, and he was consid-
erably burned. After this the fire began
to subside, and Tom stood gazing at the
scene, with Philip's books in his hand,
like one bewildered. Philip too stood
there with folded arms, looking with a
sad, sad face at the ruins of his home—
his mother's little all consumed in an
hour. Harry was trying to comfort him,
but Philip could not be comforted. Presently Hardy came up, with blackened
face, and his hand tied up in his handker-
chief. "Look here, Quin, I found these,"

said he as he put the books and the miniature into his hands.

"My books," cried Philip, "and papa's
likeness! Oh, Hardy, how did you get
them? My mother will be so pleased to
have this again. How can I thank you?"
and his conscience smote him as he remembered his sinful feelings on the previous day.

"Why, Hardy," said Harry, "you're
hurt. Did you get burnt? What's the
matter?"

The boy looked very white, and turned
away, muttering, "It's nothing—never
mind. I'm glad I got them." But Philip
followed him.

"Let me see your hand, Hardy; I'm
sure it hurts you very much. I am so
sorry." Hardy winced as he tried to un-
bind his hand. He felt happier, in spite
of the pain, than he had done, but he
could not stand Philip's thanks.

"I say, Quin, leave it alone," said he, "I'll see to it when I get home."

"But you do n't know what to do," cried Harry; "come along with us, and I'll get my mother to bind it up for you. She knows all about burns."

"No, no," said Hardy; "there's my father, I'll go home with him."

"Hollo, youngster," said Mr. Hardy, when he saw his son, "so you came after all. I thought you would n't be long after me. But what's this you've been after—getting yourself burnt, eh? Why, what a fool you must have been to get into the thick of it that way. But never mind, never mind, lad," added he, rubbing his hands, as he thought of the custom the fire would be likely to bring to his store, "it's an ill wind that blows nobody good." So saying, Mr. Hardy and Tom went on their way.

CHAPTER VII.

PHILIP'S DISCOVERY.

"Hush, idle thoughts and words of ill,
    Your Lord is listening ; peace, be still."

"Be sure your sin will find you out."

As soon as it was light next morning,
Philip, who could not sleep after the excitement and fatigue he had undergone,
went down to reconnoitre the scene of
the fire.   Nothing remained of his little
home but blackened and still smoking
embers.   It was a sad sight, for Philip
knew that with the house his mother had
lost her all.   It had always been his
comfort hitherto, that at least her home
was her own ; and he had looked forward
to the happy day when, by his own exer-
tions, he might be able in some measure
to repay her tender care and love for

him. Now all his bright hopes were
dashed to the ground—and in how short
a time! He felt very sorrowful as he
looked at the ruins, and at the spot where
the arbor had been. He thought of the
many happy hours he had spent there.
Would he ever be happy again? for it
seemed as though this terrible fire had
destroyed all his prospects for life. His
great ambition had been to study hard,
and by means of his education to make
his way in the world. But now, if he
continued at school, his mother would be
obliged to work. The thought was not
to be endured for a moment. No, he
must put his shoulder to the wheel, and
at once. There was only one thing open
to him: he must become a clerk in a
store; and a sharp conflict ensued between his rebellious spirit and his strong
sense of duty. While his mind was thus
occupied, his eye caught the glitter of

something lying on the ground. Mechanically he stooped and picked it up; it was an open knife, with "T. HARDY" roughly cut upon the handle. He slipped it into his pocket, intending to give it back when they next met, and the incident hardly interrupted his train of thought.

"Why, Philip, my boy," said Mr. Lynton, who had come up to him unawares, "I did not expect to find you here. I thought you were safe in bed, and that's where you should be," he added kindly, looking at his pale, wan face; "this sad business has been too much for you."

"I couldn't sleep, sir, and I thought I would come down and look at the old place again before any one was about."

"That's my reason for coming also, my boy, for we may find some clue to account for it. It's a strange business,

very strange," said Mr. Lynton, musing.
"Was the house on fire when you were
first roused?"

"Yes; I woke up quite suddenly, and
found the room full of smoke. I had
only just time to rush into my mother's
room and arouse her, and to wake Biddy,
before the flames burst in through the
roof.. You know it was at the back of
the house, sir; and by the time we got
down the engine was close by. They
had seen it at the village before we knew
any thing about it."

"And was that place your arbor down
there?" and Mr. Lynton pointed in the
direction it had been. "Was it burning then, or did it catch fire afterwards?"

"Oh no, sir, it was nearly burnt down
before I woke at all."

"Then the fire must have originated
there. Have you been in the habit of

keeping matches or any thing combusti-
ble down there lately, Philip?"

"No, sir, I am sure I never did."

"And you did not carry a lighted
candle there last night? Harry tells me
you went to fetch a book you had left
there."

"No, sir, I found the book lying on
the bench. The moon was so bright I
did not need the lantern."

Mr. Lynton was silent for some minutes. "It's my impression," said he at
length, "from all I can gather, that it
must have been the work of an incendi-
ary. It is a sad loss to your poor mother, Philip."

Philip's lip quivered. "That's just
what I've been thinking about, sir. I'm
afraid I must leave off going to school
now, and see if I can't find some place in
a store."

"Ah," said Mr. Lynton; "and were

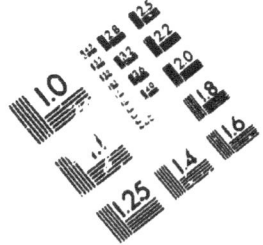

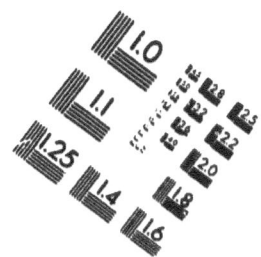

**IMAGE EVALUATION
TEST TARGET (MT-3)**

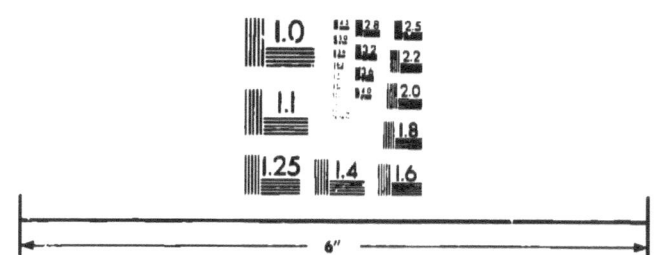

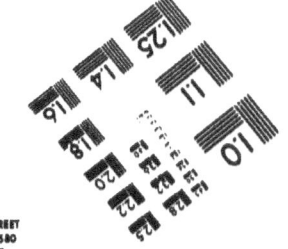

Photographic
Sciences
Corporation

33 WEST MAIN STREET
WEBSTER, N.Y. 14580
(716) 872-4503

these the thoughts that made you look so
sad when I first met you?"

"I dare say they did, sir. I am very
sorry. I did so wish to work hard and
get on in my lessons, and enter some
profession;" and Philip's voice trembled,
and the unbidden tears would start into
his eyes.

Mr. Lynton looked at him in some
surprise, for the boy had never before
spoken so openly, and putting his hand
kindly upon his shoulder, he said, "I see
this fire is likely to be the cause of even
a greater trial to you than I at first an-
ticipated, Philip; but cheer up, my boy;
you know God helps those who try to
help themselves. Besides, you must not
think it beneath you to enter a store. I
can quite sympathize with your feelings,
for you have not been long enough in
the country to understand our modes of
thought; but I can assure you that in a

colony like this, some of our most highly
educated and esteemed men have begun
life in a position such as you contemplate.
But you have not had time yet to think
over your plans; and in the meantime,
Philip, you know we are only too glad
to have your mother and you at Lynton-
·ville: and remember, my boy, you will
never want a friend while it is in my
power to help you."

"I thank you, sir, you are very kind;
indeed, I do n't know how to thank you
enough," said Philip, as they reached the
house.

Harry did all in his power to cheer
his friend. "Do you know, Philip," said
he, later in the day, when they were
talking it all over, "I 've been thinking
this morning about that text, 'Not a
sparrow shall fall to the ground without
your Father in heaven.' If God looks
after the sparrows he must know all

about this, how it happened and all, and don't you think he'll take care of you?"

"Oh, yes," said Philip, "that's what mamma says, and I don't know what we should do if we did not believe God's promises; but it's very hard to feel right about it, and to think that it's all for the best. Perhaps some day we shall know why it happened better than we can now."

Towards evening Philip slipped away quietly, to take another look at the ruins. Again and again he went over all the circumstances of the fire in his own mind; when suddenly he remembered Hardy's knife, and he took it out of his pocket. He knew it well, for he had seen it many a time before, but now it acquired a new interest in his sight. How came it in the spot where he had found it in the morning? The crowd was collected in front of the cottage, and on the bank of the river; what could Hardy have been about there? It was open too when he picked it up, as if it had just been used; and Philip examined the knife, as though the inanimate steel could give him some clue to the truth. His thoughts recurred to Mr. Lynton's idea, that the place had been set on fire purposely. Then the events of the day before flashed across his mind: the examination; the prizes he had so unexpectedly won, which Hardy had looked upon as his own; the angry scowl too upon his face, as he met him coming from the school-house; above all, the difficulty in accounting for the fire. It could not have been accidental; some one must have done it; and who was that some one?

Philip was fast working himself into a state of painful excitement. Was it possible? Yes, it was, it must have been

Hardy. He began to see it all now; this
was the cruel, cowardly revenge he had
planned, and as Philip became more and
more convinced of the truth of his sus-
picions, his angry passions rose in pro-
portion. "How wicked," he thought; "I
never injured him, that he should do such
a cruel, cowardly thing. I've borne all
his taunts; I never said an unkind word
to him in my life; and this is what comes
of it all." His brain seemed on fire, as
one argument after another to prove
Hardy's guilt arose in his mind; and his
eye gleamed with a strange light while
he pondered the facts which were so suspicious. "But this is more than I can
bear. I'll show him up in his true light;
mean, cowardly bully that he is. If it
were only myself it would be different,
but he has ruined my mother; and I hate
him. I do," said he aloud, stamping
with his foot upon the ground, "and I

should n't care if he were hung for it."
The sound of his own voice startled
him.

And was this Philip, the meek disciple
of a meek and lowly Master? It was indeed, and for a while it seemed as though
Satan had triumphed. 'All his evil passions were in league against him; anger,
hatred, revenge, all struggled for the
mastery, under the guise of righteous indignation, and a just desire to avenge his
mother's wrongs. But God, in his mercy,
will not let his children be tempted above
that they are able to bear; and so it was
with Philip. He had received great provocation. His mother, his loved mother,
had been injured almost beyond repair,
and his own prospects in life blighted;
and for what? Simply to gratify the bad
passions of a boy whom he had never
wronged. It was a severe trial, and we
must not think the worse of him because

the old self which remained in his heart
fought a hard battle with the new self
implanted by God's grace, and nearly
gained the victory; but in the hour of his
weakness he received strength from above
to resist the strong temptation. The
sound of his own voice brought him to
himself, and above the angry tumult
within his breast he seemed to hear a
still small voice, whispering, "But I say
unto you, Love your enemies, do good
to them that hate you, and pray for
them that despitefully use you, and per-
secute you."

Hitherto he had been walking rapidly
on, not caring where he went; now he
stopped, and sitting down on an old
stump by the side of the path, he took
out a little pocket Testament, and turned
to the words. The gleam faded from his
eye, and the angry look from his face, as
the holy words carried conviction to his

conscience. "Oh," he said, "how wicked I have been. I have blamed him for
the very thing I was going to do myself.
May God forgive me." A tear stole
down his cheek, a tear of repentance for
his sin, and he knelt down in the shade
of the forest-trees to pray for pardon, and
wisdom to direct. It was no easy decis-
ion he had to make. Ought he to con-
ceal what he suspected, or was it his duty
to make it known?

Very earnestly he besought his heavenly Father to guide him in the right
way, and he turned over the pages of
his little Testament to see if he could find
any message from God's word to help
him in his difficulty. Presently his eye
rested on this verse in one of his favorite
chapters: "Dearly beloved, avenge not
yourselves, but rather give place unto
wrath: for it is written, Vengeance is
mine; I will repay, saith the Lord.

Therefore if thine enemy hunger, feed him; if he thirst, give him drink; for in so doing thou shalt heap coals of fire on his head." Rom. 12:19, 20. He thought a while, and then he decided to keep what he knew to himself. "I will never mention it: God helping me, I will keep it a secret all my life." A hollow place in a tree close at hand caught his eye. "I will put the knife in there, and if it should ever be found no one will know how it came there." He had to climb up to reach it, and the knife dropped down into the cavity.

Then he turned to go home, and as he went he remembered Hardy's pale, frightened face, and how he had injured himself in saving the books. "He never could have meant to set the cottage on fire," thought Philip; "most likely the sparks were blown upon the shingles, for the wind set that way, and then the roof

caught. I dare say he was afraid of being
found out, and he must have been sorry
too, or he would not have risked getting burnt to save any thing. Poor
fellow; I'll go and ask how his hand
is by and by. Shall I tell him I suspect him? No, I think not; it will be
kinder never to let him know. Oh
Lord, help me to keep my resolution,"
he inwardly prayed, "and enable me to
serve thee aright, now and always."

In this softened frame, Philip returned
to Lyntonville. It was as though a terrible storm had passed over his soul—
the wind and the waves boisterous and
contrary, and tossing the frail bark of
his spiritual life to and fro, in their angry
tumult; but the Saviour's voice had spoken above the tempest, saying, "Peace,
be still;" and immediately there was a
calm. Oh, well is it for us all if we have
taken that gentle Saviour as our guide

and helper, that we may be enabled "so to pass the waves of this troublesome world, that finally we may come to the land of everlasting life," in the world to come.

CHAPTER VIII.

THE DAY AFTER THE FIRE.

"Conscience does make cowards of us all."

WE must now return to Hardy, whom we last saw going home with his father after the fire. As soon as he reached the house, his hand was properly bound up; his father at the same time rating him soundly for what he called his stupidity in getting burnt.

"Take care of number one; that's my maxim, lad, and you'll find it a safe one, I can tell you. But now you'd better turn in, for I should say you'd had enough of it for one night. Stay, you're cold. Come into the store, and I'll give you something to set you all to rights;" and he poured out some whisky, and made Tom drink it. It was not the first

time the boy had taken spirits, but in his
present excited state it affected him
greatly. He went up and threw himself
on his bed, and immediately fell into a
heavy sleep. It was still early when he
woke; and he roused himself with a dull
sense of something on his mind, but what,
he could not remember for some minutes.
Slowly it all came back to his memory,
and the pain of his burnt hand was only
too sure a reminder of the part he had
played in the scenes of the night. He got
up and looked at himself in the little
glass which hung against the wall. He
thought his very face would betray him,
he looked so pale and haggard; but peo-
ple would imagine it was the pain of the
burn; they could never suspect him of
having any share in it, unless—and the
mere possibility was terrible to him—
unless he had been observed going in that
direction so shortly before the alarm.

He went down stairs and wandered into
the kitchen, where the boy was light-
ing the stove before opening the shutters
in the store. He tried to whistle un-
concernedly as Jack made some common
remark about the fire, and went into the
shop.

The early morning sunlight streamed
in through the round holes in the shutters, which he attempted to take down
in the caprice of the moment, and leaving
them half-opened, went off to the wood-
shed. Here he began to cut through a
log of wood which had been left upon
the saw-horse; and then he felt in his
pocket for his knife. It was gone. He
rushed up to his room and sought for it
in every hole and corner; it was not
there. And then he remembered having cut the string which bound the little
bundle of tarred sticks with it the night
before. He must have left it in his

hurry close to the spot, and his name
cut in large letters on the handle would
be a witness against him. "Fool that I
have been," he muttered; "if I had only
thought what it would come to, I would
have seen myself far enough before I
stirred one step to do it. But there's
no one about so early as this; I may find
it yet;" and he ran off full speed to look
for the missing knife. He paused at the
ditch where he had fallen in his blind
haste before, and searched all about, but
no knife was there; and he walked on
as fast as he could to the place where
the cottage had been.

Mr. Lynton and Philip had but just
left the spot when Hardy came up, and
he saw their retreating figures crossing
the bridge. Carefully he looked about
in every direction; but, as our readers
are already aware, without a chance of
success, for it was at that moment safe

in Philip's pocket. After a long and
fruitless search, he gave it up as hope-
lessly lost. One comfort was, it was no-
where near the arbor, so that even if
found it could not rouse suspicion, and
his heart was lightened of half its load.
His chief anxiety was lest he should be
found out; yet as he stood looking at the
smouldering ruins, his conscience smote
him sorely. "I wish I'd never thought
of doing it; such a pretty little place too.
I never dreamed the fire would spread like
that; and I do n't believe any thing was
saved." No, Tom Hardy, it is easier to
do wrong than to set it right after it is
done; and that you have found to your
cost. "Well," he thought at last, "I
can't help it now, and I sha'n't care much
if I can only keep it quiet." Poor boy,
he forgot that there was One above who
knew all, and from whom no secrets are
hid. He had never been taught in his

childhood of the "Eye that never sleeps,"
resting always upon each one of us; and
now all he cared for was to escape the
anger of his fellow-creatures and the just
punishment of his fault.

As he reached his father's door, he
overheard several men talking about the
fire, and stopped to listen.

"I say, Smith, were you up at the fire
last night?" said one.

"Not I; I heard nothing of it till this
morning. They do say as how it must
ha' been a 'cendiary, and if so be it is,
they 'll put up a reward for certain."

"You do n't say so!" said the other;
"well, I was thinking myself it were
mighty strange how it comed about."

"Biddy, that's Mrs. Quin's sarvant,
told me this morning that not a bit of a
fire had been in the stove since ten o'clock
o' the mornin' yesterday, for the mis-
thress had been up to Lyntonville all the

day," said an Irish lad, who was errand-
boy and newsmonger in general to the
village.

"Aye, then I should n't wonder if
there might be some truth in it. I guess
Mr. Lynton wont let him off very easy,
whoever he is."

"Aisy is it?" said Terence; "shure
I'd flay him alive, if he was the praste
himself, for layin' a finger on the lot of
the widow and the orphan—bad luck to
him, whoever he was."

Tom Hardy shook from head to foot.
Then it was suspected. And if his knife
were to be found after all about the
place, it would prove him guilty; and
then what would become of him? All
day long the boy was tormented by these
fears, and every fresh comment upon the
fire only added to his misery. His time
hung heavily on his hands, for the school
was closed, and he hardly dared to join

any of his companions, lest some tell-tale look or unguarded word might betray him. But the days wore on; no clue had been found, and he began to be more easy in his mind. Little did he imagine that one person suspected his share in the transaction, and that person the very one he had so deeply injured.

Philip took the first opportunity of inquiring for Hardy's hand, and of thanking him once more for having rescued the books. He did it sincerely and warmly, feeling that he had now quite forgiven him from his heart for the mischief he had caused. Hardy had only meant to injure him, and for this Philip no longer harbored any angry feelings; the rest had been in God's hands. Those few kind words from Philip went straight to Hardy's conscience, and he winced under them as though each had been a lash.

"Do you know, Hardy, I am afraid I sha'n't be able to come to school any more ?"

"Not come back to school; why not?" said he in astonishment.

"Why, I must try and do something to help my mother now. I would n't have said any thing about it, only I heard that your father wanted a clerk, and perhaps he might take me." Mr. Hardy had the largest and most important store in the place, and there was no other where Philip could find employment.

"Take you into the store, Quin; do you really mean it? I thought you were too proud, a long way, to do any thing of the kind." Hardy did not now speak bitterly, but in unfeigned surprise.

"Yes," said Philip, "I have been very foolish, I know; but one grows wiser as one grows older, and I do n't know what else I can do. Do you think your father would have me?"

"I don't know," said Hardy, "he wants a man."

"Perhaps Mr. Lynton would speak for me," said Philip thoughtfully; "I think I'll ask him;" and soon after the boys parted.

So Philip wished to come into the store. Hardy was far from echoing the wish; he did not want to have a constant reminder of his folly before his eyes, but he said nothing; and the next day Mr. Lynton and Philip made their appearance.

"I believe, Hardy, you are in want of a clerk. Perhaps you would be good enough to try my young friend here, and see whether you can make any thing of him as a man of business."

Philip felt his cheeks burning; it was a hard trial for him, and one from which

"he

peak
"I
the

the
the
con-
his
next
heir

t of
good
and
g of

Mr. Lynton would willingly have shield-
ed him, could he have found any thing
more suitable at the time.

Mr. Hardy rubbed his hands, and
scanned Philip with his cold, harsh eyes.
"He's very young, sir, very young.   I
guess he wont be worth his salt for a
long time to come.   Can you write a
goodish hand, youngster? let us see;"
and he pushed the ink towards him.
Philip's hand shook so that he could
hardly hold the pen, but he managed to
write a few words in a bold hand.

"Ah, come, that's pretty well for a
beginning," said he.   "It's Mrs. Quin's
son, I believe; is it not?   A sad thing
that fire, very.   And you want to do
something for yourself, eh?   Well, sir,
under the circumstances, and since it's
to oblige you, I'll consent to try him;
but he's young, sir, far too young.   However, I'm glad to do a charitable action

at all times." Philip's blood boiled.
Did the man think he was doing him a
charity, when a word from him would
ruin his son for life? Hasty words were
rushing to his lips, when he suddenly
checked himself, and inwardly prayed
for strength to be enabled to keep his
resolution.

Poor Philip, it was no easy task he
had in prospect; but he thought of the
promise, "As thy days, so shall thy
strength be," and he was helped. It was
settled that the next Monday should see
him take his place behind the counter for
the first time, at a salary of four dollars
a week; and with a heavy heart he
walked back to Lyntonville.

"It will be a trial to you, Philip,"
said Mr. Lynton, "especially at first;
but strive to do your duty in your new
position, and you will find that God will
bless you in it. The discipline may seem

hard just now, but believe me, in after-life you will never regret it; and just let me give you one word of advice: do n't add to your mother's sorrow by telling her what a sacrifice you are making for her sake. No doubt she feels it enough already."

Philip remembered Mr. Lynton's caution, and when he told his mother of the arrangement that had been made, he did it as cheerfully as he could.

"It will be pleasant to feel that I am beginning to help you, dear mother."

" Well, my son," she replied, stroking back the hair from his forehead with her gentle, caressing hand, "it is not what I could have wished for you, but our heavenly Father knows best, we may be perfectly satisfied of that; and he is able to bring good out of what seems to us only evil."

CHAPTER IX.

MR. HARDY'S STORE.

"Teach me, my God and King,
   In all things thee to see;
And what I do in any thing,
   To do it as for thee.

All may of thee partake;
   Nothing can be so mean
That with this tincture, 'For thy sake,'
   Will not grow bright and clean."

MONDAY came, and Philip went to his post. He felt strangely awkward as he was told to assist in unpacking and marking a large case of new goods just arrived from Toronto. Hardy employed two clerks; and Bennett, whose place Philip was to take, still remained for a few days to put his successor into the ways of the business. Joe Gammon, the other, was a youth about eighteen years of age, good-looking and sharp, and unscrupulous enough in his dealings to please his like-minded master. "Joe's a lad of the right sort," Hardy used to say; "no fear but he'll make his way in the world." Bennett was an older man, and would have been a far safer companion for Philip than Joe; but he had saved money, and was now about to better himself by taking a share in a small business in a rising village a few miles off.

"You've got hold of a raw hand there, Bennett," said Joe, laughing. "Never left his mother's apron-strings before, pretty dear."

"You'll teach him a thing or two before you've done with him, I expect, Master Joe," replied Bennett. "I tell you what, youngster," added he in a low tone to Philip, as Joe walked off to the other end of the store to attend to a customer, "you'd better look to yourself here. I'm no saint myself, but of all the precious young scamps I ever came across, that chap's the worst."

There was a rough kindliness of man-ner about Bennett for which Philip felt grateful, and he was really sorry when he left the place at the end of the week. During that time he had set to work with a will to learn as much as he could of his new duties, and by degrees he became more expert, and lost his awkward ways. It was still early in the summer, and Philip used to sigh sometimes as he thought of the green shady woods, and the cool splash of the river by their little cottage. It was hot and close in the store, and the mingled odors of soap and cheese and candles and butter were often so overpowering that he was obliged to go to the door for a breath of the pure fresh air, while he leaned his aching head against the side-post. His work was very hard, and its irksomeness made it still more so; but he uttered no complaint, and even Mr. Hardy's sharp eye could detect but few faults. But he had greater trials than these. What he felt most was, being obliged to work for and with such unprincipled men as gradually he found out Mr. Hardy and Joe to be. At first he suspected nothing, for he was so conscientious himself, that it never once entered his head that they could wilfully deceive and cheat; but little by little his eyes were opened, and his whole soul revolted from such wrong dealings. Very soon Hardy's customers began to like Philip to serve them, for they found that he gave good measure, and would recommend none but the best articles, while he was always obliging and courteous.

One day an old woman drove up to the door in one of the country wagons, and alighting, popped her head into the shop. Philip was busy measuring off some print for another customer. Seeing him engaged, she went off, though Joe was standing idle; but after a while returned again to find Philip still occupied. This time she came in, but nothing would induce her to mention her wants until she could secure Philip's services.

"What can I show you to-day, Mrs. McGregor?" said Joe, all smiles.

"It's a fine day for the mowing," replied she; "I thought we should ha' had rain last night."

"So did I," said Joe. "Is it groceries you want to-day? we have a prime lot of goods on hand just now, which we are selling cheap."

"What's that stuff-piece you have over there?" said the old lady, keeping one eye on Philip.

"Ah, the blue on a green ground. Sweet thing," said Joe, taking it down. "We have just received it, with a large

assortment of goods, by the last steamer
from the old country"—it had been in
the store a year and a half—"ten yards
to a dress.   It will suit you exactly,
Mrs. McGregor; let me cut off a dress-
length for you.   Come, I'll let you have
it for six dollars; and that's less than
cost price."

"No," she said, feeling the texture, "I
do n't think I'll take it to-day;" and
looking about for something else to remark upon, she espied a little machine
at the other end of the counter.

"And what may this be, Mr. Joe?"

"Well, ma'am," said Joe, "that is the
most extraordinary little article that's
been invented this long time; but wont
you allow me to measure you off this
piece? You can't do better, I assure
you."   Then seeing Mrs. McGregor's
attention wholly diverted, "It's an ap-
ple-parer, ma'am, and will do the work

of six pair of hands in no time at all; and
all for the small sum of a quarter dollar."

"Law, you do n't say so," said she
with pretended interest; "you could n't
show me how it works now, could you?"

"Oh, certainly, ma'am, with the greatest pleasure," and he went to get an ap-
ple for the purpose.   The paring process
was only half over when Mrs. McGregor,
to her great relief, saw Philip opening
the door for the other customer, who
had completed her purchases, and suddenly leaving Joe and his machine, she
walked across to the opposite counter,
saying to Philip, "I'll tell *you* what I
want, Mr. Quin, for I believe you wont
cheat me; but as to that young chap yonder, he shall play off none of his tricks
upon me."   Joe did not like to be out-
shone thus by the new-comer, and found
ways and means of venting his spite upon
Philip, who on the whole led no easy life.

Mrs. Quin had taken lodgings in the village, in order to be near her son, and Philip went home to her every evening after the store was closed. But the close confinement soon began to affect his delicate frame, and he often longed to be at his beloved books, when he was occupied all day long in weighing out pounds of sugar and measuring yards of factory cottons for the poor settlers of the district. His mother watched his pale face grow thinner, and his step less light every day, with sad forebodings. She would have given all she had to be able to take him away from his distasteful occupation, but his weekly earnings contributed materially to their support, and what could they do without them? No repining word ever passed his lips, and even his fond mother never guessed how much he suffered.

In the mean time things went on much

as usual at the Long Cross school, though
Hardy now found a new and scarcely less
formidable rival in Harry Lynton.   In
one thing however Tom was changed, for
he never went into the store if he could
help it, and avoided Philip as much as
possible ; but all sorrowful recollections of
the injury his conduct had caused seemed
to have faded from his memory.

Harry never ceased to miss his friend.
" I declare," said he one day, "I never
see you now, Phil ; but I suppose it can't
be helped.   I do n't know how I get on
without you though, for you always contrived to keep me straight."

"You can't be more sorry than I am,
Harry," replied Philip sadly; "it seems
as if all my happy days were over.   Only
I believe it 's my duty, and that makes
me more reconciled to it."   Scarcely a
day passed without Harry making some
little errand to the store, that he might

have an opportunity of chatting with
Philip; and these short visits and the
evening hour with his mother were the
only pleasures he had to relieve the mo-
notonous labor of his life. And so week
after week passed on; but Philip remembered he was helping his mother, and
this was his greatest comfort. He scarcely knew himself how weak and ill he
was, and toiled on, thankful for the employment which helped to keep the wolf
from the door. Very often they had
to deny themselves necessaries; and it
would have melted the hardest heart to
have been an unseen witness of their
daily meal. "Mother," Philip would
say sometimes, "I'm not hungry to-day;
I can't eat any dinner;" and all Mrs.
Quin's persuasions would only induce
him to taste the scanty fare. Again, if
he happened to be later than usual, she
would keep the lion's share for her boy,

while perhaps little food had passed her
own lips that day. None knew how hard
a battle they had to fight with poverty;
and Philip tried his utmost to earn a
higher salary. Mr. Hardy knew full
well he was worth it; but while he could
secure his services for four dollars a
week, why should he think of raising it?
And the poor boy, in his inexperience
trusting to his master's honor, toiled
harder than ever to win his approbation.

September was now drawing towards
its close, and the bright autumn tints
told a tale of coming winter, when Mr.
Lynton having made arrangements for
his usual hunting expedition, determined
this year to take Harry with him, so
pleased was he with his industry and the
progress he had made at school. Harry,
nearly wild with delight, rushed into the
store as soon as he possibly could, to tell

Philip the good news.   Poor Philip's face
fell.

"Going away for a month.   Oh, Harry, what shall I do without seeing you
sometimes ? I shall miss you so much."

" Never mind, old fellow," said Harry,
" a month will soon pass, and then I
shall be able to tell you all about it, you
know.   But I say, is n't it jolly, though?"
Philip did not look as if he thought it
very jolly, but he tried to sympathize
in his friend's pleasure.   "There goes
the bell ; I came in early on purpose to
tell you, Phil, but I must be off now."

In the course of the day it chanced
that Tom was sent into the store by his
father, as an extra hand was required,
and for the first time for several weeks
he noticed Philip, who was looking more
than usually pale and weak.   "Why,
Quin," said he, "how bad you look;
what 's the matter?"

"I do n't know," replied he; "I 'm all right, thank you."

"But you do n't look all right, I can tell you. Why do n't you take something? I believe you ought to have port wine, you have n't got a bit of color in your face. Why do n't you?"

Philip smiled a melancholy smile as he thought of their narrow means. "We can't afford it," he said quietly. Hardy turned away quickly and asked no more questions. "I believe he 's going to die," thought he; "this hard work is killing him; he 's not used to it." More slowly the idea forced itself into Hardy's mind that this was his own work, and the idea once there, he could not get rid of it; it followed him wherever he went, and once he woke with a start in the night dreaming that he was being dragged off to prison, accused of Philip's murder.

Harry had been gone very nearly a

month, and Philip rejoiced much at the
prospect of welcoming him back again
so soon.   October was passing quickly
away, the trees were already leafless and
bare, and sharp frosts had set in, which
made poor Philip shiver and cough.   He
himself began to think that he should not
be able to go on much longer, for sometimes he became so dizzy he was obliged
to sit down by the roadside, cold as it
was, on his way to the store in the morning; and he felt he could not lift the
same heavy weights he did formerly.
One day when he went as usual to the
post-office for the. letters he found one
addressed to himself, and greatly to his
surprise, on opening it, he saw that it
contained nothing but a ten dollar note.
His heart was full of wonder and thankfulness as he thought of the many little
comforts this sum would procure for his
mother, and all day he tried to think who

the kind donor could be. His mother
had not seen him look so joyful for weeks
as when he threw the letter into her lap
and made her guess what was in it.

"But who can have sent this money to
us, Philip? I am afraid to use it without
knowing."

"Why, mother, surely some one who
wishes to be kind to us. Oh do spend
it," he cried, looking quite disappointed. "It must be meant for us ; for, see,
it is directed to me quite plainly."

Mrs. Quin looked troubled as she
examined the envelope. "I think, my
boy," she said at length, " we had better not touch this note at present unless we are driven to it. My heart mis-
gives me, lest there should be any thing
wrong."

Philip's bright look had quite vanish-
ed now, but he never questioned for a
moment his mother's wishes. "Well,

mother, I suppose you know best," he said, "but I am very sorry."

Mrs. Quin locked up the letter, just as it was, in her desk, and they tried to think no more about it, though that was no easy task when they needed help so much.

A few evenings after this occurrence, Philip came home so ill that Mrs. Quin felt sadly grieved. "My dear boy," she said, as he sat down at her feet and leaned against her knee, "you must not go again. See, I have been able to get some employment too," and she showed him some needlework she had been busy with when he came in. "Phœbe Harris is going to be married, and she asked me if I knew any one who could help her for the next few weeks, and I gladly offered. You know I am a famous needlewoman."

Philip looked up in mute dismay. "Oh,

mother, mother, that it should come to this. You must not do it. Indeed, indeed, it will kill me to see you working. I cannot bear it." And in his weakness and excitement he laid down his head and sobbed.

"My darling," she said, soothing his distress by her gentle tones, "you must not give way like this. Rather let us thank God that he has put this offer of work in my way. Indeed, I have been full of thankfulness ever since, for I have tried before to find employment without success; and now, Philip, I must try and do it so well that I may make a reputation," she added playfully, though her heart ached as she looked at her boy.

"Mother, God has dealt very hardly with us."

"Hush, my Philip," she said solemnly, "you must not say such words. 'Whom the Lord loveth he chasteneth.'

Our trials come from his loving hand,
and you know, dear, he can remove them
quite as easily when he sees fit." A long
time they sat thus, and talked together
as only those who are very near and dear
to each other can; and before going to
rest, they knelt together at the throne of
grace to commit all their cares and sor-
rows into the hands of Him who careth
for his children.

Philip resolved to go back to the store
on the morrow, and to ask for a week's
rest. He did not know then how very
soon his connection with Mr. Hardy
would be ended.

CHAPTER X.

THE MISSING NOTE.

"Bear through sorrow, wrong, and ruth,
In thy heart the dew of youth,
On thy lips the smile of truth."

THOUGH feeling very ill next morning, Philip managed to crawl down to the store, but he had hardly entered the door before Joe accosted him, his eyes gleaming with malicious delight,

"Oh, I say, is n't there a jolly row, that's all. Here's the 'boss' been storming away all the morning, and asking for you. I expect you 'll catch it if ever you did in your life;" and Joe shrugged his shoulders and rolled his eyes in the most suggestive manner.

"Why, what's the matter?" asked Philip, feeling rather uncomfortable,

though not conscious of having done any
thing wrong.

"Ah, that's just it; who did it, I
should like to know?"

"Well, but, Joe, do tell me what it
is."

"I like your innocence," replied Joe;
"'do tell,' indeed. Just as if I should
know any thing about it. Only I guess
you'll find out fast enough as soon as the
'boss' has done his breakfast; you'd
better ask him what it is."

Presently Mr. Hardy made his appearance.

"Oh, you've come, have you?" said
he harshly; "just walk this way; I want
to speak to you;" and he collared Philip,
and half led, half dragged him into the
little inner room.

"Look here, boy, I've missed some
money from the till, and ten-dollar notes
can't walk off by themselves. Now, do

you know any thing about it? You had better speak the truth, mind, for I'm determined to sift this matter to the bottom."

Philip stood aghast. "I, sir? I never took any money from the till. I assure you I would not do such a thing; I know nothing of a ten-dollar note. Indeed I don't think I have seen a ten"—Philip suddenly stopped, colored, and hesitated; the remembrance of the note they had received through the post flashed across his mind.

"Ha," said Mr. Hardy, seizing him roughly by the arm, "you do know something about it then, after all, you young rascal, do you? I thought as much. Come, speak out."

"Oh, sir, have you—do you ever mark your notes?"

"Mark them? Oh, you want to find out that, do you, to see whether it is

worth while to confess. You've taken
a note with my private mark on it, and
you'd like to know if you can keep it
without being detected. But I'll have
the law of you, that I will, if I find this
has been any of your doings; and if it is
marked, what then? You don't leave
this room till—"

"Mr. Lynton, sir," said Joe, opening
the door at that moment, and Harry and
his father entered. In an instant Hardy's manner changed, and he dropped
Philip's arm, who uttered a cry of joy as
he saw his friends.

"Oh, sir, Oh, Mr. Lynton," cried he,
springing to his side, "God has sent you
here, I am sure, for I am accused of
stealing, and you know I would not do
such a thing."

Mr. Lynton looked from one to the
other in astonishment.

"What's all this about, Mr. Hardy?"

"Well, you see, sir," said Hardy in a fawning tone, rubbing his hands in his usual manner, "appearances are sadly against him, and I was naturally roused. It was only to be expected, sir. Here I find this morning, counting over my receipts from the till, that a ten-dollar note is missing; and when I make inquiries, this young fellow gets as red as a turkey-cock, is confused, and hesitates; and what am I to think? It's not the first little thing I've missed lately, either."

"This is a very serious accusation, Mr. Hardy," said Mr. Lynton with some severity. "I should like to hear Quin's story."

"Oh, certainly, sir, certainly. I'm willing, I'm sure, to give the lad every chance of clearing himself; but it looks suspicious, sir, very suspicious."

"We'll judge of that presently," said

Mr. Lynton. "Hush, Harry; be silent, if you please. Well, Philip, what have you to say for yourself, my boy?" he added kindly.

"Oh, sir, you do n't believe I could be guilty of such a thing—you know I could n't. But I asked Mr. Hardy if it were marked, because—because we had one sent to us in a letter a few days ago, and I noticed a little round 'o' in the corner." "Whew!" whistled Hardy, "a nice trumped-up story that is. You do n't come over me like that, my boy." Philip took no notice of the interruption. "You can ask my mother, Mr. Lynton; we 've got the note now."

"Well, if that does n't beat all," said Hardy; "now, sir, you see I was not far wrong."

"I can't say I view the case in that light, Mr. Hardy. When do you say this letter came, Philip?"

"It was Monday or Tuesday, sir, I forget which," and the boy trembled so from excitement he could hardly stand.

Mr. Lynton thought a moment. "I shall go at once to Mrs. Quin, taking Philip with me, to ascertain the truth of this matter, for I wish to see it satisfactorily cleared up, and I beg you will follow, Mr. Hardy."

"Very well, sir; I will attend you most willingly."

Mr. Lynton's conveyance was in the village, and they drove immediately to Mrs. Quin's lodging. The widow's heart sank as she saw Philip returning at this unusual hour in company with Mr. Lynton, for she feared some new evil had happened to her boy, and she hastened out to meet them.

"We want you to settle a knotty point for us, my dear madam," said Mr. Lynton after his first friendly salutation.

" An unpleasant incident has occurred in
Mr. Hardy's store; some money is missing, and Philip has mentioned that a
note has come into your possession in an
unaccountable manner, which seems to
give a clue to the lost one."

"How thankful I am," said Mrs. Quin,
"I kept the note. Here it is, in the very
envelope it came in;" and she unlocked
her desk, and placed it in Mr. Lynton's
hands. "Although I thought it not
improbable that some kind friend might
have wished to surprise us, I could not
feel comfortable in making use of it without some further knowledge."

Mr. Lynton handed the note to Hardy,
who instantly recognized it as his own.

"That's it, sure enough," said he, "for
here's my private mark on it; and now
the question is who the thief may be,
and that to my mind is as clear as day-
light."

"And pray what is your solution of the difficulty, Mr. Hardy? for in truth I cannot see my way through the business."

"Why, it's just this, sir: the lad wants money; he takes the note, posts it to himself, and brings it home to his mother. I'm sorry to say it, ma'am, for your sake, for I dare say you knew nothing about the matter; but your son's the thief, or I'm very much mistaken."

"Oh, mother, you don't believe I could have done it? Tell me, Oh tell me *you* know me to be innocent. God knows I am. Has he forsaken us altogether?" cried the poor lad, clasping his hands in an agony of despair. "Oh, Mr. Lynton, do, do believe me. I never saw the note until I took it out of the envelope; indeed, indeed I didn't. I assure you I am speaking nothing but the truth; I never told a lie in my life."

"God have mercy upon us," said Mrs.
Quin as the hot tears rolled down her
face; "we have never seen such trouble
as this." Harry stood by meanwhile,
burning with indignation. Why did n't
his father turn the fellow out; how dared
he say that Philip was a thief? But Mr.
Lynton was too judicious to act hastily
in such a case, knowing that he would
injure rather than benefit Philip's cause;
besides, he felt that it must be thoroughly investigated, and though his belief in the innocence of the boy remained
unshaken, yet he could not but acknow-
ledge that appearances were against
him.

"You say this note has been abstract-
ed from your till, Mr. Hardy; pray has
no one else besides Quin had access to
it?"

"Well, I can't say but there has;
there's Joe and may-be Jack, if he had

a mind to steal, might find some way to get at it; but the thing is, you see, sir, that here's the very identical note, and it isn't a very likely thing that either of them would steal out of charity."

"No," said Mr. Lynton, as an idea struck him, "but it is possible that this has been done to fasten suspicion upon an innocent person. I must examine the lads you speak of at once; and, Philip, you may rest assured that your previous character will go far to clear you from this imputation in the sight of your friends, until it is proved beyond a doubt that you are guilty."

Philip had quite regained his composure; but the hot flush had faded from his face, leaving him so deadly pale that Mr. Lynton was shocked to see the change that had taken place in his appearance in a few short weeks.

"I cannot say more than I have said,

Mr. Lynton, and my mother knows it is true. We have often wanted money, and when that letter came I thanked God that he had put it into the heart of some kind friend to send it. I little thought then it would be the means of such trouble to us; and now I can only wait patiently till—" The door suddenly opened, and all eyes turned towards the new-comer. Tom Hardy, for it was he, walked straight up to his father.

"Look here, father," said he, "stop all this; do n't accuse Philip Quin of doing what you know it is not in him to do. I took the note."

"You!" exclaimed all the party in various tones of surprise; and Harry shouted, "Tom Hardy for ever!" not caring in his glee who was the guilty party. so long as Philip was cleared.

"You, you young scoundrel, you robbed your father's till!" cried Mr. Hardy, turning upon him furiously; "come along with me, and—"

"Stop, Mr. Hardy, we have a right to hear the story out; speak out, boy." Tom Hardy looked Mr. Lynton full in the face, sullen, but resolute.

"I'll tell you why I took it, Mr. Lynton. I saw Quin getting thinner and thinner; I knew four dollars a week was barely enough to keep him from starving, and that my father ought to give him more, and I thought to help him. I suppose you'll say it was wicked. I pretty nearly always am wicked now," he added bitterly; "but I can't help it. If you knew all—"

"Can't help robbing your father, you good-for-nothing boy?" screamed Mr. Hardy. "I'll teach you to say you can't help it," and he made a rush at his son as if he were going to administer summary punishment then and there.

Philip, who had sunk down on a seat by
his mother's side, half bewildered by the
sudden turn events had taken, started
up. "Oh, Mr. Hardy, do n't be angry
with him, pray do n't be angry; I 'll do
any thing if you 'll only promise not to
punish him."

"Never mind, Quin, let him beat me
if he likes; it does n't much matter. I 'm
sure *you* need n't beg for me, for I 've
only done you harm."

"Wait a while, Mr. Hardy," interrupted Mr. Lynton. "Why did you not
ask your father for the money, Tom ?"

"Because I knew he would n't give it
to me. I expected there 'd be no end of
a row when it was discovered, but I
did n't mean the blame to fall on him,"
and he pointed over his shoulder to
Philip; "I thought he would have spent
the money before now too."

"And you actually braved your father's anger, and committed this theft, to do Philip Quin a kindness?" For the first time the boy faltered and was silent.

"This is a very strange story, Mr. Hardy, and yet I am bound to believe it. I am also much pained to find that you have deceived me with regard to Quin. You are aware that before I left home some weeks ago, I had a conversation with you on the subject; and you then professed yourself so well satisfied with the lad, that you agreed to increase his salary from that date; this I find you have not done. After what has occurred to-day, if Mrs. Quin will permit me to take this matter into my own hands, Philip will no longer remain in your service; and if your word is of any value, the note is still his by rights; the arrears of his hard-won earnings for the past five weeks, and you are yet six dollars in his debt for the present one." Hardy, biting his lip to control his passion, threw down the money on the table and stalked out of the room without more ado; his son was about to follow, when Mr. Lynton held out his hand to him. "As for you, Tom, you have done very wrong, but I believe you did it thoughtlessly, and under a strong sense of the injustice done to Philip. If you come up to Lyntonville to-morrow, I shall be glad to speak to you."

When they were left alone, Harry's joy could brook no further restraints. He clapped his hands, and capered about in the most eccentric manner.

"Philip, my boy, I congratulate you," said Mr. Lynton, shaking him warmly by the hand, "and you also, my dear madam; and now I think a little change of scene and rest after all this trouble and annoyance will do you no harm; so if you will kindly put up any thing you may require,

I will come round in half an hour and drive you both back with me. Mrs. Lynton is already prepared to welcome you, for I sent off a messenger some time ago, though I hardly hoped then we should have been so cheerful."

Very shortly after, the happy party were all assembled once more in the hospitable old homestead of Lyntonville.

CHAPTER XI.

THE CONFESSION.

"I saw that I was lost, far gone astray;
   No hope of safe return there seemed to be;
But then I heard that Jesus was the way,
   A new and living way prepared for me."

THE change was so pleasant to Philip, that he could scarcely realize at first his freedom from hard work and the watchful eye of his harsh master; and when Mr. Lynton took him into his library, and pointed out a number of shelves from which he might choose any book he liked, his delight knew no bounds. Was it possible that his weary shop-boy life was over, and he had leisure once more to return to his much-loved studies? But in a day or two the reaction came, and the exciting events of the past week in

particular began to wear on his feeble
frame.

Nothing was heard of Tom Hardy next
day until Harry returned from school
with the news that he had left the village,
no one seemed to know why or wherefore.
For a time, Philip seemed to be gradually recovering; but when the severe
cold set in, and he was no longer able to
leave the house, the slight improvement
was checked, and he became very ill.
Mr. and Mrs. Lynton would not hear of
his leaving their hospitable roof, for they
knew he needed tender nursing, and
many comforts which his mother's slender
means could not afford.

"No, my dear friend," Mrs. Lynton
would say, "you know it is quite an ac-
quisition to us to have such an addition
to our party in this dreary winter weather, and Harry is so delighted at having a
companion again that it would be quite

cruel to leave him alone at present."
The widow's eyes would fill with tears,
as she thanked the kind friends whom
God had raised up for her in her sore
distress. For a dark shadow hung over
her. Her son, her only son was passing
away, as she feared, before her eyes, and
it seemed as though the light of her life
would be quenched. It became necessa-
ry soon to keep Philip a close prisoner
to his room, for the only chance of saving
him seemed to be to nurse him carefully
through the long winter, and his fond
mother clung to the hope that new health
and life might come to her boy with the
breath of the sweet spring-time. Harry
spent the greater part of his leisure with
his friend, and helped to cheer him with
his unfailing mirth and high spirits. He
never thought for a moment that Philip
was in any danger; so his merry laugh
rang out clear as ever, as he rushed into

his room with some tale of school-life,
full of boisterous glee and rude health.

One day he was running home as fast
as usual, when he saw a boy skulking
about near the house, and to his surprise
Tom Hardy came up.

"I've been watching for you this long
time, Lynton; tell me how Quin is."

"Why, where have you sprung from,
Hardy? I thought you had gone away,"
said Harry, without answering his question, and wondering at his gaunt looks, so
different from the last time they met.

"Well, you see, I'm here now, at any
rate; but I want to know, how's Quin?"

"He's very ill," said Harry, looking
grave.

"Where is he now? Up here?" said
Hardy, with a nod of his head in the direction of the house.

"Yes, they've been here ever since."

"But tell me, Lynton, he isn't going

to—to die?" said Tom, with quivering lips.

Harry looked at him with astonishment; the idea had never struck him, but he did not like it nevertheless. "No," he answered shortly, "of course not."

"I wonder if I—"

"Why, Hardy, what's the matter?" asked Lynton in surprise, for the boy was so unlike his former self that even "careless Harry" could not fail to be struck by it.

"I don't know; I'm very hungry."

"Why, man, come along; why didn't you say so before? I'll find something for you," cried Harry; "here, this way," and he led him towards the house. At the door Mr. Lynton met them.

"Tom Hardy, you here; is it possible?" said he.

"I'm going to get him something to eat, papa; he says he's hungry."

"I've had no food to-day, and scarce any yesterday," said Hardy, "or I wouldn't ask."

"Poor fellow; why, how is this, Hardy? But come in, you are not in a fit state to answer questions;" and Mr. Lynton brought him in, while Harry busied himself in getting a comfortable meal provided for his former school-fellow.

"And now, Hardy, come into the library, and tell me all about it," said Mr. Lynton, rising when he had finished. Tom followed him into the snug warm room. "I expected to see you again after the last time we met, but Harry came home and told us that you had disappeared. What happened then?"

"Didn't you hear, sir, that my father turned me out of doors? He told me that if I ever dared to come into his sight again, he would have me taken up and put in prison; so I ran away that night.

Jack managed to put up some of my
clothes for me on the sly, and I had a
little money. I walked as far as the
'Four Corners,' where the stage stopped,
and got a lift on to Midborough."

"And what did you do when you got
there?"

"Well, sir, I scarcely know how I
have lived this last two months, but I got
errands, and one thing and another, so
that I did n't starve: and a woman who
once lived about here, gave me lodging
for a trifle, and a dinner too sometimes;
but it was hard work."

"But what brought you back here,
Tom?"

The boy looked down and hesitated.
His lips were no strangers to a lie: but
Philip's life had not been without its ef-
fect upon him. He had been kept from
stealing many a time, when sore pressed
by hunger, by the memory of his patient

endurance; and now he had been drawn
back to the neighborhood chiefly by a
rumor of Philip's serious illness, which,
had reached him by chance at Midborough. He felt he must confess, for the
weight on his conscience was more than
he could bear. Philip might be dying,
and he must ask his forgiveness before it
was too late. Mr. Lynton's kind words
too had not been thrown away, and he
did not fear to meet him again, but he
was not prepared to unburden his mind
to him. He could not tell Mr. Lynton
why he was there without betraying his
secret. Mr. Lynton, surprised at his con-
fusion, repeated his question.

"I—I want to see Quin," he blurted
out at length.

" Well, you shall see him presently,"
said Mr. Lynton kindly; "but what are
you going to do with yourself afterwards?"

"I do n't know; going back, I suppose," said Tom rather dubiously.

" Well, I must see what can be done; perhaps I may be able to find some employment for you. Come in," he added, as Harry knocked at the door.

" Philip wants to see Hardy, papa, when you have done with him."

" You can go now, Tom," said Mr. Lynton; and Harry led the way to the room which Philip occupied. The sofa on which he was lying was drawn towards the window, and the pale crescent of the new moon shone in in the cold grey twilight of a winter's afternoon. Philip held out his wasted hand as Hardy entered, and Harry left them together. "I 'm sorry you 're so bad, Quin," said Hardy, looking frightened and pale, and beginning to repent of his resolution to confess—it seemed so much more difficult, now that the time had come.

"I wanted so much to see you, Hardy; you do n't mind coming up, do you? I've been ill, and sometimes I think I shall never be any better; and I thought I should like to give you this," said Philip, laying his hand on the Bible by his side, which Mr. Elmslie had given him, and Tom had saved from the fire. "See, I · have written your name in it; and, Hardy, you will keep it and read it for my sake, wont you?" he added earnestly. "Dear Tom, will you promise me?"

"Oh, I can't, I can't have it," sobbed the boy, quite broken down by Philip's pleading words. "I 've done you more harm than any one else ever did, and I can't—I can't."

"Oh Hardy, you will? It is the last thing, most likely, I shall ever ask you, and you wont refuse me? I know you will not."

Tom rose from his low seat by Philip's

side, and calming himself, spoke rapidly
and with a strong effort.

"Stay, you don't know all; wait till
you hear, and then you will hate and despise me as I hate and despise myself
now; but I must tell; I came here to
tell you, for I can't keep it to myself any
longer, and I don't care what becomes
of me. I burnt down your place there,
I did, because I hated to see you getting
the prizes and keeping above me in the
class. Do you hear?" said he, seeing
Philip looked neither surprised nor indig-
nant; "I tell you 't was I set fire to your
arbor that night. I did n't mean to burn
the cottage, but it caught. It was I that
ruined you, Quin, and brought all this
trouble upon you; and if you die, I shall
feel I have killed you: and now you
know all." His forced composure gave
way, and hiding his face in his hands,
he sobbed as if his heart would break.

There was silence in the room for a minute, broken only by the sound of Hardy's weeping; and then Philip laid his hand gently on his arm.

"Dear Hardy, I have known all this a long time." The boy looked up in blank amazement. "Yes," continued Philip, "I suspected it from the very first, and I'll tell you why. Do you remember losing your knife about that time?"

"Yes," said Hardy, "and I searched and searched for it again and again."

"Well, I picked it up where you had dropped it that night, and I have ever since been pretty nearly sure that you did it. I let the knife fall into the hollow tree up by Long Acre afterwards."

"And you never told?"

"No," said Philip; "I was very angry at first; but then I thought how it was— that it was worse than you meant it to

be ; so I have always kept the secret.
I did not mean to tell you now, only you
spoke yourself."

"Oh, Quin, how could you? And you
worked so hard, and were accused of
stealing too, when you knew it was all
my doing; and you never spoke a word."

"I prayed that God would help me,
Hardy, and he did. I was very near
telling two or three times though. If I
had not had strength given me, I should
have done so."

"But, Quin, why did n't you speak up?
My father would have been obliged to
make it all straight; and besides, you 'd
have had your revenge."

"I have had my revenge," said Philip
smiling; but Hardy broke down again.

"Oh, Quin, if I had only known. I
believe you are really good; I do. But
I 've been taught to sneer and scoff until
I scarcely know right from wrong. To

think that you should have known it all
the time, and never spoke. Oh, I wish
I could be good like you, I'm so miserable: but I never shall be; I'm too
wicked for that; and I've got a fit punishment for burning you out, for now I've
no home to go to. I wish I were dead,
that I do."

"Oh, Tom, do n't say that," said Philip; "it makes me shudder to hear you
speak so wickedly. Think what a solemn thing it is to die. Are you ready
to appear in the presence of God, and to
give an account of all you have done in
this world? Dear Tom, you have confessed your fault to me, but let me ask
you, have you ever thought of confessing
your sins to God, and asking him to pardon you for Christ's sake?"

"No," said Tom, "I never thought of
that, Philip; you know I was not brought
up as you have been. We were never

taught much about God, except in our lessons at school, and I tried to think as little of them as I could after they were said. I did not think God would care for what I did."

"God cares for all, dear Tom; he not only made the world, he rules it too. 'His eyes are in every place, beholding the evil and the good.' He sees all that we *think*, as well as all that we *do;* he hears every word we say; and he has said that not only for every evil deed, but for 'every idle word that men shall speak, they shall give account in the day of judgment.'"

Tom looked up anxiously at Philip. "Then what is to become of me?" said he; "I have been so wicked, and have done so much evil. You are happy, Philip; you have always been good; you are sure to go to heaven; but what is to become of me?"

"I am not good, Tom ; and if I could get to heaven only by my own goodness, I should never get there at all. I feel that I am a sinner, that there is no good thing in me, and my only hope of being .saved is through what our Lord Jesus Christ has done for us. He died on the cross to save us poor sinners. I trust in him alone ; and he will save you too, if you ask him."

"I learned that at school," said Tom, "but I never thought much about it. I did not think then that I was a sinner. I had not done any thing very bad till I burnt your house, and you know, Philip, that I did not mean to do such a wicked thing : I only meant to burn the summer-house ; and you could easily have built that again. But somehow, ever since then I seem to have been going from bad to worse. I am bad enough now, I feel that. But still I think you have been good, Philip; you have been an honest boy and a good son."

"Even if my outward conduct had been quite good," said Philip, "which it has not always been, still my heart has been wicked. Sin ruled in my heart by nature, as it does in the heart of every unrenewed sinner; and though I trust that I am pardoned for Christ's sake, and I strive against sin as a thing he hates, yet I feel daily need of forgiveness, and pray daily that God would grant me his Holy Spirit, to purify my heart and keep me from evil."

"What do you mean by 'every unrenewed sinner?'" asked Tom.

"Every one who has not become a new creature by having his sinful nature changed by the Holy Spirit, and his sins washed away by the blood of Christ. All need this change, and none can be saved without it; for our Lord himself has said, 'Except a man be born again, he cannot see the kingdom of God.'"

"But will God change my heart?" said Tom; "am I not too bad to become really good now?"

"Our Lord Jesus Christ welcomes all, even the worst, even the chief of sinners. He says, 'I am not come to call the righteous, but sinners to repentance;' and 'him that cometh unto me I will in no wise cast out.' You will find many such promises in God's word. That's why I want you to have my Bible; it's God's message to us, you know, and it teaches us what we must do. You will read it, wont you? and then you will love it as I do."

"Well, I will for your sake; otherwise I should hate to look at it, because it was partly envy about it that made me do wrong at first. But did the Bible teach you not to tell? I do n't understand."

Philip opened his little Testament, and pointed out several passages. They sat and talked together some time, and at last Hardy said,

"I suppose I must go now, and I need not show my face to Mr. Lynton again, for you 'll tell now, Philip?"

"Oh, Hardy, do tell yourself, you will feel so much happier; I 'm sure you will."

"Well, but Mr. Lynton said he would try to help me, and he wont do it if I tell; but if you do n't mind keeping the secret, Philip, as you have done for so long," and a gleam of hope brightened his face, "perhaps he will; and I 'm half starved now."

Philip looked troubled. "It would n't be right, Hardy, indeed it would not. You must tell him, and I know he wont be angry, for he is so kind. Oh do, please do tell him yourself."

"But, Quin, I can't; he 'd be so awfully angry. I'd much rather go away and shift for myself."

"He wont be angry, Hardy; and if you like, I'll tell him for you, if you stay here; Oh do let me."

"But your mother, Philip, and all of them, they will never forgive me. No, let me go away; I can get on somehow. They think I'm bad enough as it is, without this."

"No, they will not; I wont let you go away, Hardy. Mother," he cried as he heard her light step in the adjoining room, "come and sit down here by me a little while. Here's Tom Hardy; I know you'll be glad to see him;" and very gently, and little by little, he helped Hardy to make his confession. Mrs. Quin was much astonished as the truth dawned upon her; but his evident distress and sorrow disarmed every feeling of resentment, and only thankfulness for

the noble conduct of her boy remained.
Mr. Lynton was told the whole story;
and though he spoke very seriously to
Hardy, it was not in displeasure, nor did
he retract his promise of endeavoring
to find him some suitable employment.
Hardy could never forget Philip's kindness, or the earnest, pleading words he
had spoken. The memory of that inter-
view will remain with him till his dying
hour; and from that time he became an
altered character. We do not mean that
he suddenly became good and pious and
unselfish, but that day was the turning·
point in his life; and Philip was the
instrument, in God's hands, of working
this happy change in one hitherto so
unpromising.

Suitable occupation was eventually
obtained for Tom, but not before he had
been reconciled to his father, through the
kind intercession of Mr. Lynton; but Mr.

Hardy having expressed a wish that he should have an opportunity of gaining experience elsewhere before settling again in Fairfield, Tom returned to Midborough, where he remained some years. Happily he fell into good hands, and as time advanced he was enabled, by the grace of God, to overcome the disadvantages of his early associations. If we take a glance into the future, we shall see that he has so far gained the esteem and approbation of his fellow-citizens in a commendable and successful career, that if circumstances do not belie the expectations of his most sanguine friends, he will yet be a member of the Legislative Council of his country.

CHAPTER XII.

CONCLUSION.

"Be still, sad heart, and cease repining ;
Behind the cloud is the sun still shining."

"Weeping may endure for a night, but joy cometh in the morning."

MARCH had set in with hard frosts and keen, biting winds, but every one rejoiced that the long winter was nearly over; and as Philip seemed no worse than he had been for some months, hope began to grow strong in his mother's heart. But the doctor shook his head.

"I fear the month of May more than any thing for him," he said one day to Mrs. Lynton; "the sudden changes of our climate are so trying to patients of this class. A sea-voyage might save him; but I've not said so before, for in

Mrs. Quin's circumstances it must be out
of the question."

Philip, who was inclined to be rather
desponding by nature, had long given up
all hopes of recovering; and his most
sorrowful thought was of the parting with
his mother, and leaving her to fight the
hard battle of life alone.   Often they
would read together the descriptions of
the heavenly land to which he seemed
to be hastening, where there would be
no more sorrow or parting, and where
tears would be wiped from every eye.
But the parting was not so near as Philip
and his widowed mother feared, for the
chastening hand which it had pleased
God to lay upon them so long was about
to be removed, and brighter days were
in store.

Not many days after Dr. Ford's last
visit, a large packet of letters which had
arrived by the last English mail was

brought in and laid before Mr. Lynton,
as the custom of the house was, when the
party were all assembled at breakfast.
Every one was soon occupied in reading
his own, when a sudden exclamation of
surprise from Mr. Lynton attracted the
attention of all.

"Well, this is passing strange; indeed, I may say providential. My dear
madam, let me congratulate you most
warmly," said he, rising and shaking
hands heartily with Mrs. Quin. "I have
good news for you. I am informed that
your son, Philip Walter Quin, has just
fallen heir to the property, real and per-
sonal, of his uncle Capt. W. P. Quin,
who died suddenly on the tenth of April
last. A long and fruitless search has
been made for him, and now this letter
is sent to me as the magistrate of this
district, making inquiries concerning the
whereabouts of the said Philip Quin,

who is supposed to be living somewhere in the neighborhood, as his presence is required at once, if possible, in England. I think," he added smiling, " I shall be able to give the requisite information."

Astonishment took the place of every other feeling in Mrs. Quin's mind at these unexpected tidings.

"But are you sure this is true?" she said, "for one chief cause of our leaving Ireland, and our consequent troubles, was an unhappy quarrel between my husband and his brother, and any hopes of help from that quarter I had entirely given up for years."

"Nevertheless it is undoubtedly true," replied Mr. Lynton, "for here are full particulars from his solicitor."

Mrs. Quin took the letter; but her eyes were blinded by the fast-falling tears, as she thought that if this good

news had only come in time, her son
might have been spared to her.

"Oh," cried Mrs. Lynton, when she
understood it all, "how thankful I am. It
was only the other day Dr. Ford told me
that a sea-voyage might yet save Philip,
and I believe it will." The widow caught
eagerly at her cheering words, and when
the doctor came in later in the day and
confirmed her most sanguine hopes, her
joy and gratitude to the gracious Giver
of all good things knew no bounds.

"But you must break it to him very
cautiously," said he, "for any great excitement in his weak state might prove
fatal; and the greatest care will be nec-
essary in the land journey. Once get
him to the sea, and there is not so much
to fear."

It was some time before the widowed
mother could realize her happiness, for
she hardly dared to believe that her be-

loved son might yet be spared to her.
As she grew accustomed to the idea, and
felt that their bitter days of poverty
were over, her joy seemed almost too
great.

"How can I ever thank you, my dear,
kind friends, for all you have done for
me and mine?" she said. "Without
your generous sympathy, our life would
indeed have been sad—strangers and
poor in a foreign land; but God will
reward you."

No one rejoiced more unfeignedly in
the welcome tidings than Harry, and he
showed his glee in the most characteristic manner. It was all they could do to
prevent his rushing up to Philip at once,
and telling him the whole story in his
excited way; but as this was strictly and
seriously forbidden, he was obliged to
content himself with fidgeting in and out
of his room, and continually bursting out

into little bits of ecstacy, rubbing his hands and muttering to himself, "Oh, is n't it jolly?" Then, suddenly remembering that a weighty secret was entrusted to his keeping which he was on no account to divulge, he would try to look grave and pull on a long face, until the next happy thoughts of his friend's good fortune would set him off again. It must be confessed that all this was rather trying to the young invalid, who being unacquainted with the cause of his odd behavior wondered what could possess his light-hearted companion. But Harry's patience was not destined to be put to a very severe test. Towards evening, Mrs. Quin went up to sit with Philip in the twilight, as was her wont; and for a few moments after her first loving inquiries they were silent, his thin hand resting in the warm, loving embrace of hers.

"God has been very merciful to us,

12

my darling," she said softly at length, as
he leaned his head against her.

"Yes," he answered; but he spoke
sadly, for he was thinking of the parting
which seemed so near. Then he looked
up in her face, as the flame from the
open stove glanced upon it in the dim
light, and he saw that, though her eyes
were glistening with tears, it wore a joyful expression. "What is it, mother?
something has happened."

"I have just received the news of
your uncle Walter's death, Philip."

"Oh, mother; but that does not make
you glad, does it?"

"God forgive me," thought she, "I
have been selfish in my joy. No, my
boy," she said aloud, "though I never
saw him; but, Philip, it alters our circumstances very much."

"Oh, I am so glad, so thankful. Now
I shall die without a care, if I think you

are provided for. God has indeed been good to us;" and the tears rolled down his face.

"Yes, darling; and suppose you were to get well, Philip; suppose it were now in our power to use the only means of doing you good."

"Mother," said he, "you would not say so if you had not good hopes: tell me, Oh do tell me; is it true?"

"My son, in God's great mercy I believe it is," she replied solemnly. "I would not, you know I would not, be so cruel as to raise false hopes; but Dr. Ford assures me that a sea-voyage may yet restore you; and now, thank God, we can go."

"Oh, I am thankful, mother, dear mother. It would have been hard to part; but if I am spared, may God give me grace to live more to his glory, and to be a greater comfort to you than I have been." The room grew darker and dark-

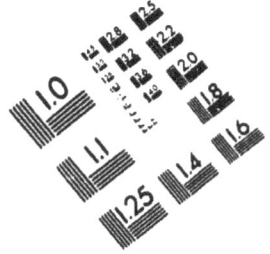

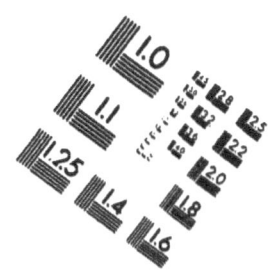

**IMAGE EVALUATION
TEST TARGET (MT-3)**

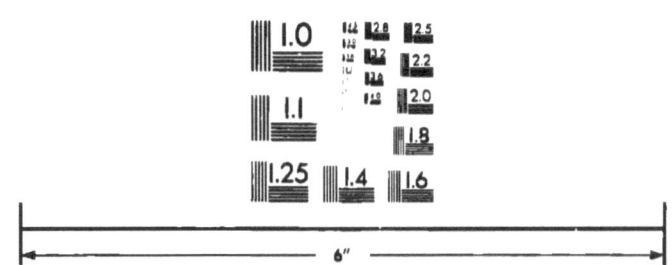

Photographic
Sciences
Corporation

23 WEST MAIN STREET
WEBSTER, N.Y. 14580
(716) 872-4503

er, but there was light and joy in their
hearts, such as they had not known for
many long days; and the mother and
son rejoiced together in their great happiness.

Little more remains to be told. Mr.
Lynton had been long wishing for an opportunity of sending Harry to finish his
education in England, and though his
parents were grieved at the thought of
parting with him, yet they would not lose
so good an opportunity; so it was ar-
ranged that he should accompany Mrs.
Quin and Philip. Great care was taken
of the young invalid, and they reached
Quebec by short and easy stages. The
journey did not try him so much even as
they expected, and with the first breath
of sea-air came a change for the better.
They arrived in Liverpool after a pros-
perous voyage, and soon after proceeded
to London, where Harry sorrowfully

bade them farewell before entering alone upon the new and varied experiences of an English public school.   He often missed Philip's ready advice and help, and right glad was he when they met again once more.   It was in Mrs. Quin's pleasant country residence that his happy holidays were spent.   Here was his second home, and he loved to call it so.

Philip by this time had regained even more than his former health, and when Harry's holidays were over, he returned with him, to contend once more for the double honors of class and play-ground. The discipline of their early days was not lost upon either of them, and Philip especially never regretted the lessons of self-dependence and self-sacrifice which he had been taught in the stern school of adversity.

And is there no truth that our young readers may learn from the little story

we have related? We think there is.
The word of God tells vs that "none of
us liveth to himself." Each word and
action of even the very youngest must
exercise some influence for evil or for
good on those around him; and we have
seen how Philip's quiet, consistent conduct was the means, in God's hands, of
leading one who seemed in every way
most unpromising, to seek for pardon and
peace through our Saviour Christ, who
alone can bestow it.

The work which God gives each one
of us, young and old, to do, lies close to
our hand; and though the path of duty
is sometimes rugged and steep, calling
for patient self-denial, yet if we strive by
God's grace to go straight forward in it,
he will surely make use of our silent ex-
ample for his own glory and the good of
those about us.

Years after, when Philip revisited the

scenes of his boyish trials, and once more renewed his acquaintance with his old companion and former foe, Tom Hardy, now become a good and worthy man, he was able to look back upon his early discipline with thankfulness, and to feel that it had not been in vain that so many of ʰis early days had been spent in the forest shades of

LYNTONVILLE.

Beautiful Books

FOR CHILDREN AND YOUTH

AMERICAN TRACT SOCIETY, 150 NASSAU-STREET,
NEW YORK.

Flowers of Spring-time. Combining amusement and instruction in most attractive forms. One hundred and fifty Engravings. Quarto size.

Home Scenes. An elegant small quarto for the family, with fourteen photographic pictures, fac-similes of fine Engravings.

Views from Nature. Forty scenes in nature and art. Finely printed in tint.

Songs for the Little Ones at Home. Attractive as ever. Beautifully illustrated.

Lullabies, Ditties, and Tales. Original short Poems for the Children, containing Tales, Songs, and Dialogues. With eighty-four Engravings.

Home Pictures. 72 pages. A fine Cut on each page.

My Picture-book. 64 pages. Sixty-one Engravings.

Fireside Pictures. 64 pages. With a Cut on each page.

The Illustrated Tract Primer. The Children's favorite. Finely Illustrated.

FOR SALE AT 150 NASSAU-STREET, NEW YORK; 40 CORNHILL, BOSTON; 1210 CHESTNUT-STREET, PHILADELPHIA; 75 STATE-STREET, ROCHESTER; 103 WALNUT-STREET, CINCINNATI; and in other cities and principal towns.